THE MERMAID BRIDE
and
other Orkney Folk Tales

II

THE MERMAID BRIDE
and
other Orkney Folk Tales

Told by Tom Muir
Illustrated by Bryce Wilson

The Orcadian Limited (Kirkwall Press)

© 1998 Tom Muir and Bryce Wilson

ISBN 0 9526174 2 0
Hardback

ISBN 978 0 9526174 3 3
Softback

Printed and Published by The Orcadian Limited, (Kirkwall Press),
Hell's Half Acre, Hatston, Kirkwall, Orkney, KW15 1DW

Acknowledgements

There are many people who have helped in the production of this book, and to them I would like to offer my sincere thanks. Firstly I would like to thank the former Head Librarian, Bobby Leslie, and all the staff of the Orkney Library, without whose help and cheerful support this book would have been much thinner. As well as a wonderful library we are fortunate to have an equally wonderful Orkney Library Archives. A huge thankyou to Archivist Alison Fraser and her assistant Phil Astley for supplying me with endless boxes and reels of film.

A special thankyou to John Fergusson and all the team at BBC Radio Orkney for letting me use recordings from their archives, and giving me cups of coffee.

Thanks also to Stromness Museum for drawing my attention to the George Marwick papers in their archives, and to Ron Marwick for giving his blessing to my using his great-uncle's work. The School of Scottish Studies at Edinburgh University for letting me use their archive recordings. The Orkney Library Archives for access to the Ernest Marwick papers. James Miller and all the staff at *The Orcadian* for their help, and for having faith in this book. Morag Robertson for pushing me in the right direction. Peter Leith for his helpful information on standing stone lore. Beatrice Thomson for her blessing on my using her father's stories. Sorcha Cubitt who read the book in its early stages, and whose enthusiasm made me think that there was a need for this book after all. Elizabeth Bevan who read the text and made some much needed corrections. To my wife Karen and my children Danny and Josie who kept me going when I felt like giving up. And last, but not least, Bryce Wilson, without whom this book would never have been written, and whose illustrations bring the stories to life.

Tom Muir.

Dedication

This collection of tales from the past I would like to dedicate to my children, Daniel and Josephine Muir (Danny and Josie).
May it bring joy to both old and young alike.

Contents

Introduction	XI
The Creatures of Orkney Folklore	XIII
Assiepattle and the Mester Stoor Worm	3
The Caithness Giant	10
Why the Sea is Salt	12
The Mother Of The Sea	14
How the Mermaid Got Her Tail	15
The Trows of Trowie Glen	16
The Lost Girl	19
The Selkie Wife	21
The Fin Folk and the Mill of Skaill	23
The Standing Stones	25
Jock in the Knowe	28
How Tam Scott Lost His Sight	30
The Rousay Changeling	34
The City at the Bottom of the Sea	36
The Selkie Man	45
Tam Bichan and the Trow	47
The Giants of Hoy	51
The Shetland Fin Wife	53
The Hogboon of Hellihowe	55
The Everlasting Battle	57
Lady Odivere	59
The Trowie Snuff-Box	65
The Suiter from the Sea	66
The Sandwick Fairies	68
The Water Trows	69
Hilda-Land	70
The Changeling Twin	74
The Holms of Ire	76
Mansie O' Fea	77

Kate Crackernuts	79
The Changeling	82
The House Of The Dead	83
The Death of the Fin King	84
The Fairies Fishing Trip	89
The Broonie of Copinsay	90
The Good Neighbours of Greenie Hill	94
The Fairy Battle	95
The Breckness Mermaid	97
Davie O' Teeveth	99
Building The Cathedral	101
The Stolen Winding Sheet	102
The Evie Man's Dance	108
Boray Isle	109
The Trows of Huip	112
Hether Blether	113
Tammy Hay and the Fairies	115
The Nucklavee	118
The Fairies and the Vikings	121
The Bride of Ramray	122
The Trow's Curse	125
Peerie Fool	127
The Trow Wife	132
Ursilla and the Selkie Man	133
The Dancers Under the Hill	135
How the Fin Folk Lost Eynhallow	136
The Midnight Ride	141
The Selkie Wife of Westness	142
The Farmer and the Trow Servant	146
The Man From Nowhere	148
The Dead Wife with the Fairies	150
The House on Sule Skerry	151
The Death of the Mainland Fairies	153
The Mermaid Bride	154
Appendices	161
Notes and Sources	177

Introduction

The winter sun had passed beyond sight, and darkness spread over the land. The people had fed their animals and closed them in for the night. Inside the broch the fire burned brightly in the centre of the room, casting shadows on the wall, that twisted and danced. The long winter nights were ideal for telling stories, and all the eyes in the room were turned towards the old man with the long white beard as he began to speak. They had heard all his tales before, but he had the gift to turn his words into colourful pictures in the imagination of all who listened to him. His story was a well-known one, of how the fairies had stolen a baby and replaced it with one of their own, a spiteful little creature with a cruel heart. They all knew where the fairies lived, and they avoided those places. But the people now had iron to protect themselves, and they were not so frightened anymore.

Generations passed, and the Vikings found these green islands off the northern tip of Scotland, so different from the lands they knew. The Picts who lived here spoke a strange language that the Vikings could not understand. One man had learnt to speak the Viking's tongue, the first of many to do so. He told them the tales that were told to him when he was a child. Of the beautiful mermaid who lured away a man from a house by the shore, never to be seen again. And of the selkie folk who swam in the sea for most of the year but who could throw off their skins and dance in human form when the tide was at its highest. In the Viking longhouse the men feasted by the long fire that ran down the middle of the room. As the ale flowed the old saga man stood up to recite the stories of the kings of old, and the jarls who fought great battles and won riches and land. The children who were playing by the door ran to an old woman sitting in the corner spinning wool. "Granny, tell us that story of the Ash Raker who kills the Stoor Worm."

Orkney's folktales are as old as the prehistoric houses that grace our islands. They were told for hundreds, even thousands of years, until they were stamped out in the name of progress. Science explained the things that we could not understand. Archaeology has answered many questions about the ruins that lie hidden in the mounds, once the homes of the fairy folk. We forget that the creatures in the stories were once as real to people as the fish in the sea or the birds in the air. If we forget our folklore then we are in danger of losing an important part of our heritage. For the first time ever, the folktales of Orkney have been brought together in one book. No doubt there are other stories that are still lying hidden on book shelves, or half forgotten in people's memories. This collection is as much as I can discover, and has taken many years to find. Some of the stories are familiar, others not so. Many of the tales are published here for the first time. It is time to read these stories to our children, and our children's children. We live in the computer age, but surely there is still room for magic and wonder in our lives.

Tom Muir, November 1997.

The Creatures of Orkney Folklore

CREATURES OF THE LAND

Fairies/Trows

The word 'trow' comes from the old Norse word 'troll', meaning a supernatural creature. In Orkney the word has been mixed up with the fairy, so it is hard to say if we are dealing with one or more type of creature. In the text of this book I have used the name given by the person who told the story.

The fairy/trow varies greatly in size, from the tiny to not much smaller than a human. They were usually small, though very powerful. They could steal a newborn baby and replace it with one of their own sickly brats. The baby was not the only one at risk, for they would also take a woman who had just given birth. She would then have to act as a wet nurse to a fairy child. The woman was replaced by an object, like a log of wood. It was made to look just like her by fairy magic, and it would seem that the woman had died in childbirth. The best form of protection was an open bible left in the bed and steel, usually a knife, above the bed or door. Cattle too were taken, leaving a similar substitute lying 'dead' in the byre. When old people became senile they were thought to have been taken by the fairies. This condition was called being "in the hill". Duncan J. Robertson remembered the story of ". . . a very old man in Rousay was very angry with his son and daughter because they would not bring him back "out of the hill," though he told them the very spot where they would find him."

Fairies/trows made their homes in mounds, usually the sites of Neolithic chambered tombs or Iron Age brochs. These mounds were best avoided, as the trows could shoot people or cattle who got too near. They fired 'elf shot', which could cause great pain or even death. Neolithic flint arrowheads found in fields were thought to be 'elf shot'. and were kept as a charm to protect the owner from harm.

Fairies/trows enjoyed music and they loved to dance. People entering into the mounds where they live joined in the fun for what seemed like a few minutes. On leaving the mound they found out that they had been inside it for a year, or even longer. The fairies were thought to live outside of time as we know it. It is interesting to note that the American writer Washington Irving, who wrote the story of Rip Van Winkle who fell asleep for thirty years, had an Orcadian father. William Irving was born and brought up at the farm of Quholme on the island of Shapinsay. He left home as a young man and went to sea.

Fairies/trows were at their most powerful at certain times of the year. Midsummer and midwinter and Halloween were times when extra care had to be taken. They rode on horses, stolen from the stables of their mortal neighbours, but they were equally at home riding through the air on bulwands (dock stems). For longer journeys between islands straw ropes, called simmans, were used. It was unlucky to throw an eggshell into the fire without crushing it first, for the fairies would use it as a boat. When at sea they had the power to sink the first ship that they met.

Hogboons

Hogboons take their name from the old Norse 'Haug Bui' meaning mound dweller. They lived in a mound next to a house, and could bring luck to a family if they were treated with respect. Offerings of food were left on the mound for the benefit of the hogboon. They seem to have a particular tie with one specific family, leaving their mounds to follow them to a new home.

It was once the custom for bride's-to-be to have their feet washed before the wedding. A laird's daughter in the seventeenth century had her feet washed in wine instead of water. The wine was drunk by some of the servants, not for the love of the wine they protested, but for love of the young lady. The housekeeper was very annoyed about it saying "I meant to pour the wine on the house-knowe, whar the hogboon bides, for good luck to the wedding."

Giants

For a group of islands that are as flat as Orkney, there seem to have been enough hills to hide giants. The most famous of all the Orkney giants was Cubbie Roo. He was actually a real person, Kolbien Hruga, who lived in the island of Wyre in the 12th century. His castle can still be seen there, and he appears in the Icelandic Sagas. The Orkney giants were in the habit of throwing stones at each other, and many large rocks were pointed out as some of these missiles. Giants were also keen bridge builders, but they enjoyed little success. Long rows of stones going out to sea are said to be the result of some unsuccessful bridge building from one island to another.

CREATURES OF THE SEA

The Fin Folk

There was a race of men who lived under the sea called the Fin Folk. The men had dark complexions and wore fins that were wrapped around the body to look like clothes. The fins were also concealed by the Fin Folk's magic, for they were powerful sorcerers. They travelled about in boats which they propelled with oars, never a sail. With the power of their magic they could travel from Orkney to Norway or Iceland with just seven strokes of the oars.

The Fin Folk used the fishing grounds around Orkney. If a human trespassed on one of these grounds he was liable to attract the wrath of the Fins. The unsuspecting fisherman could have his boat attacked during the night, a small hole being made where it would not be seen until it was too late. Oars may also have been broken and fishing gear destroyed. To safeguard against attack the fisherman could paint a cross on the side of the boat. The heathen Fins were afraid of this, and would not go near it.

Fin folk were very fond of human woman, and there were many tales of young girls being carried off from the shore by them.

Mermaids and Fin Wives

The Fin Folk's women were mermaids, the most beautiful creatures to live on land or in the sea. The typical mermaid of folktales has a fish's tail, but the Orkney variety were said to be different. Walter Traill Dennison recorded an argument between the old men and old women of Sanday on this point. The old men said that the mermaid had a fish's tail, while the old women said that they were 'foolish' and that the mermaid wore a beautiful petticoat of silver and gold that could be closed over the wearer's feet when she was in the water.

If a mermaid gripped the bow of a boat and asked the state of the tide, a wrong answer had to be given. If the man gave her the correct answer she then had power over him, and could pull him and his boat under the sea.

Mermaids were also fond of getting a human husband, and with good reason. If they married a Fin man they were doomed to lose their beauty, becoming old and haggered. But if they married a human, they could keep their dazzling looks forever.

If a mermaid married a Fin and lost her beautiful looks, she was known as a Fin wife. Many of these old women went to live on land and acted as witches. They sold good winds to sailors, and sent the money home to their Fin husband. Fin Folk loved silver, or white money as it was called. If a human was ever hired to do a Job by a Fin man, he would always be paid in coppers.

The Homes of the Fin Folk

The Fin Folk had two homes, one under and one above the sea. Their home under the waves was Finfolkaheem, a beautiful place with houses made from coral and studded with gems.

Their home above the sea was called Hilda Land, meaning hidden land. It took the form of a lovely green island, usually invisible to the human eye. It could become visible every now and then, but soon faded from sight. Another name for this magical abode was Hether Blether, and it was often seen by Rousay folk lying out in the Atlantic, to the west of the island.

Nucklavee

The Nucklavee was the most horrible of all the creatures who lived in the sea. Its name means 'Devil of the sea' and its hatred of mankind knew no bounds. The story in this book gives a good description of the monster, so I will say no more. I will just add that when seaweed was first burnt for kelp in Orkney, on the island of Stronsay, the smell greatly offended the Nucklavee. As a punishment it unleashed a deadly disease called 'Mortasheen' amongst the horses of the island.

Selkie Folk

It was thought that seals, called selkies in Orkney, had the power to take human form during certain times of the tide. There were two different stories about how selkie folk came into being. One was that they were angels that had been cast out of heaven for some unknown offence. The crime was not so bad as to see them being sent to hell, but they were forced to live as seals in the sea. The other version is that they were the souls of people who had drowned. Some said that it was only suicides who turned into seals. Both stories agree that they had the power to throw away their skin and dance in human form at certain times of the tide. The selkie folk were thought to be very lovely looking, hence the young man's desire to carry away the selkie girl as his bride.

Sea Trows

There was a race of trows who lived in the sea. They had been driven there by the more powerful land trows, but they always wanted to return to the shore. They were described as having a face like a monkey and a head that sloped like the roof of a house. It was covered in scales and its hair was like seaweed. Its oversized limbs and round feet made it an ugly beast, though it was quite harmless.

It was very lazy and tried to steal fish from fishermen's hooks. Sometimes it only succeeded in hooking itself and was brought to the surface by the horrified fishermen. There are no stories about the sea trow that I have found, but the creature in 'The Broonie of Copinsay' fits the description in many respects. There are recordings of "water trows" living in freshwater lochs.

Water Horses

Water horses haunted freshwater lochs and burns. They looked like lovely strong horses, and came in many colours. They tried to get unwary humans to climb up onto their backs, and they would carry them into the loch and drown them.

THE MERMAID BRIDE
and
other Orkney Folk Tales

Assipattle and the Mester Stoorworm

here was once a farmer who lived on a fine farm called Leegarth. It lay in a valley surrounded by hills, and a burn danced down the hillside past the house. The farmer lived there with his wife and seven sons. They all worked hard on the farm, all that is except the youngest son. He would do no work but lay by the fire, raking through the ashes. That is how he came by his name, Assipattle. His ragged clothes and tangled hair were always covered in ash so that if there was any wind the ash would blow from him like smoke from a fire. His father and mother shook their heads when they looked at him sitting by the fire. His brothers hated him, they would kick him and curse his laziness.

One day terrible news reached Leegarth, the Stoorworm was drawing near to their land. This was the Mester Stoorworm, the oldest and most terrible Stoorworm of them all. The other Stoorworms in the sea were his offspring, but they were not as destructive or evil as their father. Where he came from nobody seems to know, but it was said that he was created by the Devil. He was so big that he could sweep a whole town or hill into his mouth with his forked tongue and swallow it in one gulp. He could use the forks of his tongue to seize his prey. The highest castle or the loftiest ship could be cracked open like a nut and its contents swallowed. If the earth shook or the sea flooded a field it was the Stoorworm yawning. He had grown so big that he had to curl his body right around the earth. His foul breath could kill every living thing it touched. Its stench swept over the countryside like a disease. Of the nine fearful curses that plagued mankind the Stoorworm was the worst.

When the Stoor Worm arrived at the country where Assipattle lived it began to yawn. That meant it had to be fed or it would destroy the whole land. The king ordered a meeting of all his advisers to try to decide what they should do. After some time they suggested that the king should seek the advice of a spaeman who had the reputation of being the wisest man in the kingdom. The spaeman was brought before the king and asked for help in ridding the land of the Stoorworm. The spaeman thought for some time, then said there was a way to please the Stoorworm. Every Saturday, when the Stoorworm awoke, they must feed him seven young maidens. This was the only way to stop him from destroying all the land. So each Saturday seven young girls were given to the Stoorworm for breakfast. This caused great sadness throughout the country as one by one the young girls were taken from their homes and families.

One Saturday the goodman of Leegarth went with his wife and sons to the top of a hill to see the Stoorworm eating his breakfast. The seven girls were bound hand and foot and laid on a rock by the shore. When the Stoorworm awoke he picked up each girl between the forks of his tongue and swallowed her whole. It was an awful sight, and the old man and his sons grew pale when they saw it. The old man said that there must surely be some other way of saving the land than this. Then up spoke Assipattle: "I will willingly fight the monster, I'm not afraid of it!" His oldest brother kicked him and told him to go back to his ash hole. All the way home Assipattle boasted that he would kill the Stoorworm, until his brothers grew tired of him and pelted him with stones.

That night Assipattle's mother sent him to the barn to tell his brothers that supper was ready. When Assipattle came to the barn his brothers were threshing straw for the cattle's supper. They threw him on the floor and piled straw on top of him. Assipattle would have smothered if his father had not come in and saved him. At the supper table the father was scolding his sons for what they had done. Assipattle said to his father that he had not needed his help as he could have beaten them all if he had wanted. "Then why didn't you try?" sneered one of his brothers. "I wanted to save my strength for when I fight the Stoorworm." said Assipattle. All his brothers laughed at him, his father shook his head.

"You'll fight the Stoorworm when I make spoons from the horns of the moon." he said sadly.

The death of so many young girls was causing a great outcry in the country. The king called the spaeman to him once more and asked if there was not some other way of being rid of the Stoorworm. After some time the spaeman said that there was indeed one other way, but it was too terrible to say. The king ordered him to speak and with a trembling voice the spaeman said that the only way the monster would depart was if it was given the most beautiful girl in the kingdom, the king's only child, Gem-de-lovely. The blood drained from the king's face and he stumbled back to his chair. "If that is the only way, then so be it. It is surely a wonderful thing that the last of the oldest race in the land, who are descended from the great god Odin, should die for her folk."

The king asked that his daughter should be spared for three weeks so that a proclamation could be sent throughout the land. If anyone would fight and kill the Stoorworm, then they would receive his daughter's hand in marriage. As a wedding gift the king would give to the brave knight his kingdom and his famous sword Sikkersnapper that had been handed down through the family from Odin himself.

Thirty six champions gathered at the castle with many a brave word on their lips. Their brave words soon turned to ashes in their mouths when they saw the monster they were expected to fight. Twelve of them fell sick at the sight of the Stoorworm and had to be carried back home. Twelve others ran away. The twelve knights who remained were no better than the others. They skulked about inside, drinking the king's wine and saying little.

The night before the battle was due to commence the knights were in worse spirits than usual. The king looked at them with contempt. He was old, but the blood of an earlier and nobler race flowed through his veins. He decided to strap his sword Sikkersnapper to his side and face the monster himself. He had a boat made ready and he waited for the dawn.

At Leegarth all were in bed. Assipattle lay by the fire listening to his parents quarrelling. They were talking about going to see the fight that was to take place between the king and the Stoorworm. The old man said that they would ride his horse, Teetgong. Now this horse was the fastest horse in the land, but it had a secret. What made the horse run so fast the woman wanted to know. The old man was loath to tell her the answer to this, and that was why they were quarrelling. After some time the old man said he would tell her, but she had to keep the secret. To make Teetgong stand as still as a rock you had to pat him once on the left shoulder. To make him run fast you had to pat him on the right shoulder. To make him run as fast as the wind you had to blow through the thrapple[1] of a goose. When he heard that sound, there was no horse in all the kingdom that could come close to him. He said that he kept a

---

[1] *Windpipe*

goose's thrapple in his coat pocket for that purpose. The old man bade his wife goodnight and they went to sleep.

Assipattle heard all this, and when he was sure that they were asleep he went to his father's coat and took out the goose's thrapple. He sneaked out of the house and went to the stable. He tried to take Teetgong, but the horse reared and kicked for he knew that this was not his master. Assipattle patted the horse's left shoulder and it stood still. He climbed on its back and patted it on its right shoulder. Teetgong set off with a loud neigh that woke the whole house. The father and his sons took horses and went after Assipattle and Teetgong shouting, "Stop, thief." The father rode fastest and was catching up with them. He shouted out aloud,

"Hi, hi, ho!
Teetgong wo!"

When Teetgong heard this he stopped, but Assipattle took the goose's thrapple from his pocket and blew it with all his might. When Teetgong heard that it took to its heels and ran so fast that Assipattle could hardly breathe.

When Assipattle reached the coast it was almost dawn. He found a small croft house in a valley nearby, and tethering his horse he slipped inside. An old woman was lying in bed, snoring loudly. The fire glowed softly, for it had been rested for the night with damp peats. He found an old iron pot and placed in it a live burning peat from the fire. The old woman never heard him, but her grey cat yawned and stretched itself at the foot of her bed.

He then headed for the shore where the king's boat was lying at anchor. A man was on guard, standing in the boat. He was grey with cold. Assipattle greeted him with a cheery smile, "Why don't you come ashore and warm yourself?" he shouted. "I can't," said the man, "if the king's kemperman caught me he would beat me black and blue." "You'd better stay then, a whole skin is better than a sackful of sore bones! As for myself, I'm going to light a fire to cook some limpets for my breakfast." With that Assipattle began to dig a little hole in the ground to make a hearth for his fire.

"Gold, gold, it's gold!" shouted Assipattle, "There's gold in this earth, see how it shines!" On hearing this the man jumped out of the boat and pushed Assipattle aside. Assipattle ran to the boat and cast off, still carrying the pot with the peat in it. When the man realised he had been tricked it was too late and he jumped around the beach with rage.

The head of the Stoorworm looked like a lofty island in the middle of the bay. Its round eyes were like two deep dark lochs. When the morning sun touched the monster's eyes it would begin to wake up. It always gave seven huge yawns before it woke, then its forked tongue would sweep out to grab any living thing within reach. Assipattle hoisted the sail and headed towards the monster's head. As he looked around he could see the king and his men on the beach, dancing with rage.

The sun rose from behind the hill and its first rays kissed the Stoorworm's eyes. The monster opened its huge mouth and yawned. Assipattle steered the boat along the front of its mouth, and waited. When the Stoorworm opened its mouth once more the water rushed in like a waterfall. Assipattle's boat was carried into the monster's mouth with the water and went right down its throat. On and on, down and down the boat went, deeper and deeper into the Stoorworm. The inside of the Stoorworm was like a cave with openings on either side. Some water ran down this way, some ran down that way, until the river along which Assipattle sailed grew shallower and shallower. The inside of the Stoorworm was not at all dark, but glowed with a soft phosphorescent light.

At last the boat grounded and the mast stuck into the roof of the passageway. Assipattle took the pot in his hand and waded and ran as fast as he could until he found the Stoorworm's giant liver. He took out a knife and cut a hole in the liver and placed the burning peat in the hole. He blew and blew and better blew on the peat until he thought his head would burst. At last the oil in the Stoorworm's liver caught fire, and it spluttered into flames. It soon was blazing away like a Johnsmas bonfire. Assipattle did not have any time to waste. He took to his heels and ran for all that he was worth back to the boat.

The Stoorworm was starting to feel sick. It retched and retched until it brought up all the water that had run into its stomach. Assipattle's boat was carried along with the huge rush of water, right out of the

Stoorworm's mouth. Assipattle, boat and all were cast up high and dry.

The king and all the people on the shore thought that the world was coming to an end. They all ran up a hillside as fast as they could. The king, the man that was in the boat, and the old woman, who had been woken by her cat, all gathered together where Assipattle was standing. Smoke could be seen coming from the Stoorworm's nostrils so that the sky was filled with darkness. In its dying agony the monster shot out its huge tongue. It reached so far up in the sky that it caught hold of the moon. It nearly pulled the moon down, but the fork slipped over the horn of the moon and came crashing down to earth. It fell with such force that it made a huge hole in the earth's surface. Water rushed into it and that cut off the lands of Denmark from Norway. The hole the Stoorworm's tongue made is now called the Baltic Sea. The two great bays at its end are the forks of the Stoorworm's tongue.

As it died the Stoorworm raised its head a great way out of the sea. It fell back down to earth with such a crash that it knocked out some of its teeth and these fell into the sea and formed the Orkney Islands. It raised its head for a second time, again more teeth flew out when it crashed back down and these are the Shetland Islands. Once more it raised its terrible head and the teeth lost this time formed the Faroe Islands. The Stoorworm then curled up its huge body into a great lump and there it remains to this day, only we call it Iceland. The fire that you see there dancing from the mountains is the liver of the Stoorworm, still burning.

The king took Assipattle in his arms and called him his son. He was given the hand of the Princess Gem-de-lovely, and they fell in love. The king strapped the sword Sikkersnapper to Assipattle's side and told him that the kingdom was his. They were married in great style and lived in happiness and joy, and if they are not dead they are living yet.

The Caithness Giant

There was once a giant who lived in Caithness. One day he decided that he wanted some earth and turf. Whether he wanted it to enrich his land or for building a turf wall, I don't know. He looked over the Firth and saw good land in Orkney, and he thought it would do him just fine. He picked up his caisie,[1] and off he went. He was so tall that he could wade through the Pentland Firth like it was a duck pond. He soon came to a good spot and slung the huge caisie from off his back. He scooped up a handful of earth, leaving a large hole in the ground. After tipping the earth into the caisie, he scooped up another huge handful of earth. This was also tipped into the caisie, till it was quite full. Water began to pour into the two holes that the giant's hand had made, and these became the Harray Loch and the Stenness Loch.

Slinging the caisie onto his huge back the giant set off for home, quite pleased with himself. As he started to wade back through the sea, a turf fell from the top of the caisie. There he left it, and there it remains as the island of Graemsay. On he went until disaster struck! The fettle of the caisie broke, and down fell the whole load. The giant left in disgust, never to be seen again, but his load of earth remains to this day for all to see, as the hills of Hoy.

[1] *A straw basket carried on the back like a rucksack. It is held in place by a rope called a fettle that passes around the wearer's chest.*

Why the Sea is Salt

Long, long ago, when Christ was just a boy, there was a time of peace throughout the world. The most powerful king in the north lands was King Frodi Fridleifsson. King Frodi ruled Denmark, and the calm period of his reign was known as the peace of Frodi.

King Frodi travelled to Sweden to see King Fjolnir. When he was there he bought two giant maidens called Fenia and Menia from King Fjolnir. It was at that time that a giant quern called Grotti was found in Denmark. It was so big and heavy that no one in the land could turn the stones. This quern was no ordinary hand mill though, it contained magic powers. It could grind out whatever it was ordered to. King Frodi wanted gold, so he set the two giants, Fenia and Menia, to work grinding gold from the mill. The giant bond-maidens ground out gold both day and night. They also ground out peace and happiness so that it was a wonderful age to live in.

After turning the quern stones for some time, Fenia and Menia grew tired and asked King Frodi for a rest from their labours. The king replied that they could only stop for no longer than the cuckoo held its peace or a song might be sung. Angered by their master's response, the giant bond-maidens started to chant a strange song called "The Lay of Grotti". While they sang they ground out an army to challenge Frodi, and bad luck for the land. That same night a sea-king called Mysingr sailed to Denmark and killed King Frodi. Then the peace of Frodi was ended.

Mysingr took the magic quern Grotti, and Fenia and Menia, and sailed away. He bade them to grind salt for him on the magic quern, so the giants ground salt for the rest of the day. At midnight they asked Mysingr if he was not weary of salt yet. He told them to grind salt for longer still. Around and around went the quern until the ship was filled with salt, and it sank beneath the waves. Fenia and Menia still grind salt at the bottom of the sea, and that is why the sea is salt. There is a whirlpool now over the spot where the quern Grotti lies. It is caused by the water falling through the eye of the millstone as it turns. This whirlpool is in the Pentland Firth, and is called the Swelkie.

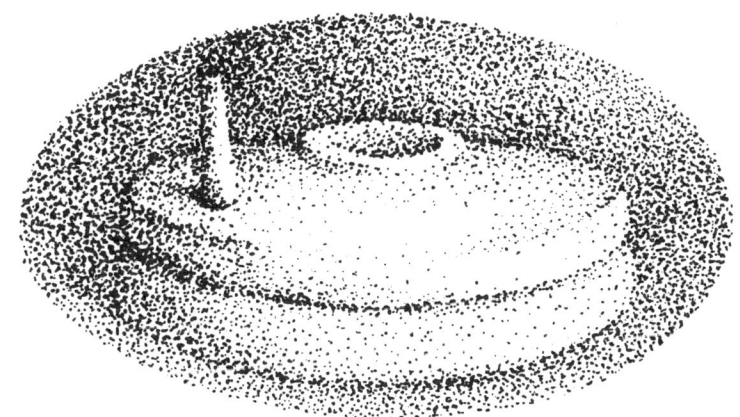

The Mother Of The Sea

he sea is guided by spirits. They are invisible to mortal eyes, but are as real as you or me. The Mother of the Sea gives life to all the creatures that live in the deep. She calms the seas in summer, and gives the fisherman his means to make a living.

She had a rival though, a black hearted monster called Teran. He causes the storms that cast ships onto the rocks and floods the land. He rules the sea in the winter, and is the enemy of mankind.

Every year the Mother of the Sea and Teran fight a great battle for control of the deep. Their fighting causes the storms that whip up the sea to foam during the spring. This battle is called "the Vore Tullye" (spring struggle). The Mother of the Sea defeats Teran, and binds him in chains. He is set on the ocean floor, and there she guards him. Now in the summer her reign begins and the sea is fruitful and warm.

As the year grows old, so the Mother of the Sea grows weak from all her work. Teran begins to struggle to break free from his bonds. He escapes, and the two old enemies do battle once more. Their fighting causes the autumn storms known as "the Gore Vellye" (harvest destructive work). Teran wins the battle over the weakened Mother, and she is driven from the sea to exile. Now Teran causes havoc, and his winter reign begins. The Mother of the Sea wanders the earth until the spring when she is strong enough to challenge Teran to another battle, and bring calm to the seas once more.

How The Mermaid Got Her Tail

he mermaid was the first created, and was the most beautiful of all creatures. One day a great queen, they say it may have been mother Eve herself, was bathing in the sea. When she stepped out of the water she saw the most beautiful woman sitting on a rock. It was the mermaid, but in those days she did not have a tail. She was naked, and sat combing her hair and singing.

The queen was amazed to see such beauty, and shocked that the woman wore no clothes. She sent one of her maids over with a dress for the mermaid to wear, but she refused, singing,

"I am queen of the sea, and mermaid's my neem,
Tae shaw my fair body I denno tink sheem.
Nae claiths file my skin, nae dress will I wear,
Bit the braw taets[1] o' me bonnie, bonnie hair."

The queen was filled with rage and Jealousy. She got all the women in the land to cause a great fuss about the mermaid. They said it was a sin to let a creature as beautiful as the mermaid sit naked on the shore. They also complained that she was so lovely that no man would ever look at them while she was around. They said that her beauty came from magic and her music from enchantment. They demanded that she should be doomed to wear a fishes tail.

The men of the land added a ray of hope for the poor mermaid, and it was this. If ever a mortal man should fall in love with a mermaid, then she should have the power to lay aside her tail. It was done, and that is why the mermaid has a tail, and why she is so keen to find a human husband.

[1] *A small bunch of something that can be held in the hand.*

The Trows of Trowie Glen

ansie Ritch lived at Rackwick in the island of Hoy. Its rocky shore, bounded on either sides by tall red cliffs, looks south over the Pentland Firth. One night Mansie was walking home over the old hill track after a visit to the north side of Longhope. All was well for the first hour of the journey, but soon he was overcome by a strange feeling. He was being drawn by some mysterious force to the head of Trowie Glen. At first he tried to fight it, but it proved too strong for him, so he thought it best to allow himself to be guided. When he reached the head of the Glen he discovered that he was not alone. A procession of peedie[1] folk, not more than a foot high, were all heading in the same direction. The procession stopped at a cave that was about half way down the Glen. The leader spoke to Mansie, saying, "You stay here a minute until I see if 'Himself' will see you."

Mansie was a little bit scared by this time, but he was determined to find out more about the peedie folk, and especially about the one they called 'Himself'. After about five minutes another trow came to the door and beckoned to Mansie to enter. Trembling with fear, Mansie entered the doorway. Much to his surprise he found himself in a beautiful large hall hung with tapestries of the most lovely design, but the most fabulous of all were the rich furnishings. Couches and divans made from the finest of wood filled the room, which was carpeted from end to end. A dance was in full swing, but Mansie was shown to a smaller side room to wait for 'Himself'. He had not long to wait for a door opened, and in came a person dressed in the finest of clothes. He was a bit taller than the others, about eighteen inches high Mansie thought, and had a white pointed beard. He was dressed in pale blue velvet and wore a blue turban

[1] *Small.*

of the same material on his head. Two of the peedie folk carried a throne into the room, and "Himself" sat down. "Boy, do you know who I am?" he asked. "Never a bit of me knows who you are," said Mansie; "But faith boy, I'm not scared of you all the same." "Well said!" said 'Himself', "you're a brave man to come into my palace. I'm the head child here in the Trowie Glen, and before you can come this way you must have a pass with my name on it. I'll give you one before you go. But you must have a drink of ale with me, boy, you never tasted ale like it."

'Himself' called to one of his servants to bring a tankard of heather ale for his guest. "Try you that boy," said the king; "and if you have tasted better stuff, you can call me a cheat!" Mansie thanked the king, and drained his glass. The ale had its effect on Mansie, for he felt as light

on his feet as a feather. He joined in the dancing with the trows, much to their delight. There were about thirty couples on the floor. All the little ladies were dressed in white and Mansie thought that they were the most beautiful thing that he had ever seen. As he danced everyone applauded him, though the dances were not ones that he had ever seen before.

He felt so at home among the peedie folk that he asked the king's permission to light a pipe. "Himself" granted his request, and they all gathered around to watch this strange ritual. Mansie filled his old clay pipe with Bogie Roll, a very strong type of tobacco. He lit his pipe and happily blew the smoke out in large clouds around his head. He had no sooner done this than a terrible thing happened. All the peedie folk turned a ghastly white and fell choking to the floor. The last of all to succumb to the fumes was the king. As the peedie man in blue fell over, Mansie found himself outside once more. He was lying in front of a rabbit hole in Trowie Glen with not a trow in sight.

The Lost Girl

here was a once a family who lived in the North Isles, a father and mother with two sons and a daughter. One day the daughter was sent to gather limpets for bait, but she never returned. Her family searched high and low, but there was no sign of the girl.

Years later the father and his two sons went fishing. It was a fine day when they left, but soon they were wrapped in a thick fog and had no idea which direction was home. After a while the boat beached on an island shore. The three men left the boat and followed a path that led to a beautiful house. They knocked on the door, and it was answered by a handsome man. He invited them in, saying that they could stay until the fog cleared.

The men gasped at the sight of all the beautiful furnishings in the house, it was even grander than the laird's house. The man introduced them to his wife who was none other than the lost girl. She welcomed her father and brothers warmly, asking after their health and that of all her folk back home. Her husband asked his father-in-law if he had any cattle to sell. He said that he did have one fine cow that he could have, and the man paid well for it in gold sovereigns. Now the old man thought that he could find out what island they were on. He said, "Well, you'll have to tell me now how to get here, or I'll not be able to take the cow to you." "Och," said the man, "Don't you worry about that. I'll come for the cow myself."

One of the brothers said that the fog was lifting and they should be on their way. The girl asked: "Is there anything in the house that you would fancy to take home with you?" Her husband said, "Oh, your welcome to anything that's here, just pick anything you would like and take it with you." The girl gave them a hopeful look, thinking that her father would choose her. But his eye had fallen on a large golden plate, and he took that home with him instead.

As they pushed the boat back down to the sea the man said, "Just pull that way a bit." and they headed into the bank of fog. As they came out the other side they found themselves near their own island. When they reached their own home they found the old woman very agitated. "An awful thing's happened," she said, "our best cow's lying in the byre dead." But the old man smiled, saying, "Ach, let her go, she's well paid for." The island, the man and girl were never seen again.

The Selkie Wife

arly one spring morning a young man was walking by the shore in Deerness. He had gone down to see if there had been a ware brak[1] during the night, and if the beach would yield a good supply of seaweed. Other people thought that he was probably coming home from the lasses, but I couldn't say.

The sun was just peeping over the horizon as he walked along the shore. It was then that he heard a sound that surprised him very much. Around the corner from where he was he could hear fiddles playing and people laughing and dancing. He crept close to the cliff and looked around the rock that jutted out from the banks. The sight that met his eyes made his hair stand up on end with fright. A group of people, about a score he thought, were dancing around in a circle on the beach, and they were all naked. The music was being provided by three fiddlers who sat on large smooth rocks. Near by them was a pile of seal skins that shone like silver in the first glint of the morning sun. He knew that they were not humans, but selkie folk.

The laughter and screams of the women soon made him feel at ease, and he crept into a hollow in the rocks to watch them dance. As the sun rose in the sky the music stopped and the people all went to their seal skins and started to slip them on and head for the sea. One of the skins was lying near to the young man, and he made a grab for it and ran around the corner of the rocks. He saw all the selkie folk in the water, all now in their selkie forms. All that is except for one young woman. She ran around the shore searching for her skin, and she shivered with fear. At last she ran around the corner of the cliffs, right into the young man's arms. He seized her tight and dragged her up the beach. She struggled like a wild animal, shouting and screaming in the selkie tongue, for the selkie folk have their own way of speaking.

She scratched him, she beat him with her fists, she bit him, but he would not let her go.

What his mother had to say when he returned with a naked girl under one arm, and a seal skin under the other, I don't know. But the young man was enchanted by her beauty, for all the selkie folk are good looking. For two or three weeks she sat by the fire crying. After a while though she started to settle in well. She soon picked up the habit of wearing clothes and she learnt how to speak. She worked around the house and was soon a great favourite of the old woman. The young man was as enamoured with her as he had always been, and she seemed to be fond of him too. She would never let him out of her sight for a single moment. At last they were married, and people said that she was the most beautiful bride that Deerness had ever seen.

The young man had locked her selkie skin away in a big kist,[2] and hid the key. She said that this was for the best, as she had put her seal days behind her. They lived together in happiness for years and had bonnie bairns together.

One day the man took his children to Kirkwall to visit the Lammas Fair. The selkie wife was left behind at home and thought that she would use the time to clean and tidy the house. While she was at work she accidentally came across the key of the kist. How she found the key of the kist is a mystery, for she had not been looking for it. She stood for a time fingering the key. She knew what it unlocked, and what lay inside, waiting.

When the family returned that night there was no sign of the woman. The lid of the great kist stood open, and the skin was gone. Maybe the temptation of seeing her old skin had been too much. When she saw it, it must have been tempting just to feel it on her back again, just one more time. The urge was too great to bear and her old life called her back to the waves.

The selkie wife was never seen by the man or their bairns again. I have heard it said that on a bonny summer's evening when those bairns were down at the shore playing, a selkie would swim in close to the shore in front of them. It would stay there the whole time that they were playing, and it would sob like its heart was breaking.

[1] *When seaweed is cast ashore.*   [2] *Chest.*

The Fin Folk and the Mill of Skaill

In the West Mainland parish of Sandwick lies The Bay of Skaill. There was a water mill down by the shore where the people of the district went to have their corn ground into meal. The mill had attracted the attention of the Fin Folk who lived in the waters nearby. They would come out of the sea at night, terrify the miller, then carry off all the meal to their halls under the sea. The miller eventually had enough and closed the mill. It stood empty for three years, not a soul was willing to take it on.

One day an old beggar woman came to the district seeking alms. She went from house to house, but always got the same story; there was no meal to give. She asked the people why the mill was closed and they told her about the Fin Folk and their thieving ways. She said that she would try to rid them of the Fin Folk if they wished it. They said that they did, so the old woman set about carrying out her plan. She told them that all she needed was fire, a cooking pot, water, some kail and a ladle. She said she would also need a spinning-wheel. Everything was brought to her and off she went to the mill. She kindled the fire, put the pot of kail on to boil and sat down to spin.

The Fin Folk were fishing in the bay when they saw a light coming from the mill. Thinking that the miller had returned, and that there would be more meal to carry off, they swam for the shore. About a score of them headed up the beach towards the mill. When they entered they were surprised to find a solitary old woman sitting spinning. They thought that this was a trick, so they went off in search of the hidden meal. One of them stayed behind to speak to the old woman. He sat down beside her at the fire and asked her what her name was. "My name is Sell in the Mill"[1] answered the old woman. No sooner had she said this than she took up a ladleful of boiling water and kail from the pot and threw it over the Fin man's legs.

The Fin man was badly burnt and ran out of the door screaming with pain. His cries frightened the others, and they all ran to the door for dear life. When they got out they asked the Fin man who had hurt him. "It was Sell in the Mill" he said. They replied, "If Sell did it, let Sell sail away in the waters with it." They went back to the sea, and were seen no more at the Mill o' Skaill. The miller returned and started to grind meal again. They hung a caisie by the door of the mill to receive the meal that the people of the district would leave for the old woman by way of a thankyou. She was never short of food from that day until the day she died, and she never had to beg again.

[1] *Myself in the mill.*

The Standing Stones

During the Stone Age great standing stones were erected. There could be a single stone on its own, or stones set in a ring like the Stones of Stenness and The Ring of Brodgar. After their purpose became lost in the mists of time stories grew up around them and the magic with which they were associated.

The Walking Stones

Near to the Loch of Scockness in Rousay stands the Yetnasteen. Its name means the giant's stone, and like other giants it is fond of a drink. Every Hogmanay night as the clock strikes twelve the Yetnasteen leaves the place where it stands throughout the year. It walks down to the loch, covering about three hundred yards in just two giant strides, and it drinks from the loch. After it has quenched its thirst it returns back to its post where it remains for the next twelve months.

The Stone of Quoybune in Birsay also likes a drink at Hogmanay. On the stroke of midnight it silently leaves its post and walks down to the Loch of Boardhouse and dips its head into the water. After it has had its fill it returns to where it had came from, and there it remains for another year.

It was considered dangerous to try to see the stone moving and people kept away. One young man from Glasgow had heard of the walking stone and decided he would stay near to it all of Hogmanay night to find out one way or the other. As the hour of midnight drew near the man started to feel very uneasy about the task that he had set himself. He paced to and fro for a while until he discovered to his horror that he was now between the stone and the loch. As he stared at the great stone he thought that he saw it move. Fear robbed him of his senses, and he fell to the ground unconscious. His friends found him in the grey light of dawn lying in a faint. Slowly he came around, but could not tell his friends if the stone had moved and knocked him down or not.

Another tale about this stone is told. One stormy day in December a ship was cast ashore in Birsay. It was soon broken to pieces by the raging sea and all but one man was lost. The sole survivor found shelter in a cottage close by the stone. He was told the story of the stone's yearly march and wanted to see it for himself. He was warned not to risk such a venture, but he would not be told. In the final few hours of the old year he walked to the stone. He climbed up the stone and sat on the very top of it, and there he waited. What happened that night nobody can tell, but in the morning the body of the young sailor was found lying on the ground. It was thought that the stone had rolled over him on its way to the loch and crushed him to death.

Between the two stone circles of Stenness and Brodgar is the Watch Stone. It stands by the brig that crosses over the channel where the Stenness and Harray Lochs meet. It was said that this stone also drinks from the waters of the loch on the stroke of midnight on Hogmanay. It is not possible to see this stone move, as the person who wishes to will always be prevented from doing so. A newcomer to the islands was told the story by a local man and he said that he would keep watch that Hogmanay. Some time later the two men met and the local man asked if he had seen the stone move. No, said the other, something had come up and he was unable to go. Ah, said the local man, the magic still works!

Stones and Giants

There is a large single standing stone at Holland in North Ronaldsay. It has a hole in it large enough to pass a hand through, though you may not get it out again! This is the tale of how it got there.

There was an old giant woman down in the ebb gathering bait. She found a large stone slab lying on the beach and she stuck her finger through it and carried it up on land. She thrust it into the ground, and there it remains to this day.

The Ring of Brodgar is a circle of sixty stones, of which thirty six can still be seen. In the field next to it is a stone on its own, called the Comet Stone. This is the tale of how it was created.

One night a group of giants went to the field at Brodgar for a dance. The fiddler struck up a reel and away they went. They all joined hands and danced in a great circle. Round and round they went, but they were enjoying themselves so much that they never thought of how quickly the night was passing. Suddenly the sun rose behind the hills and they were all turned to stone. There they remain to this day. The fiddler can be seen standing in the field next to the dancers, for he is now the Comet Stone.

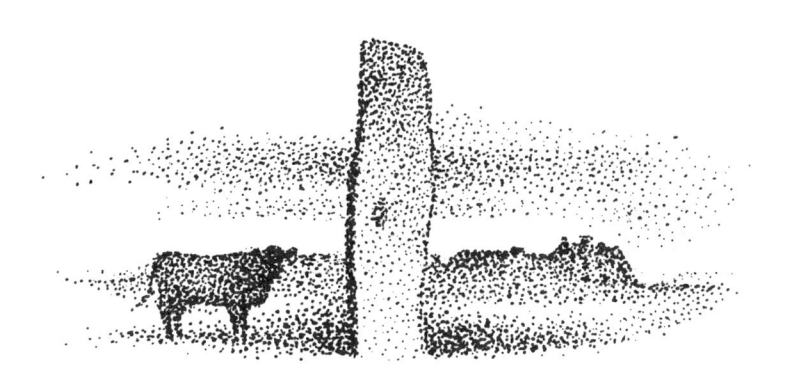

Jock in the Knowe

Two Rousay men were on their way home one evening from the fishing. The road they took went past a knowe. When they got nearer the knowe they thought they could hear music. On coming closer they could make out the sound of bagpipes coming from inside. They went around the mound, but could see nothing. Just as they were about to go, they saw a door standing open in the side of the knowe. They went to see what was inside, still carrying their heavies[1] of fish on their backs. The one man had his knife in his hand and he stuck it above the door as he went in. His companion didn't have a knife, but he went in as well.

As they stepped inside, and their eyes grew accustomed to the dark, they saw a host of fairies dressed in blue and white, dancing. The one man said: "Boy, Jock, it's time to go." He turned around, took his knife from above the door and left. His friend did not have a knife, and without steel he had no power to escape. The door closed and he was left inside. His friend got a party of men together and went to look for the knowe, but they could not find it.

A year later the same man was on his way home from the fishing once again. His journey took him on the same road as it had done the year before. Again he heard music, and found the knowe where he had lost his friend. He ran home and got two knives and an iron hoop from an old barrel and went back to the knowe as fast as he could. When he arrived he found the door, and there he saw Jock in the same place as he had left him, still with the heavie of fish on his back. He stuck the two knives above the door, entered, and threw the hoop right over Jock. As he did this the fairies all disappeared and the door closed when the

---

[1] *A straw basket worn on the back.*

two men came out. Jock thought that he had only been in the knowe for a few minutes, and it took some time to convince him that it was not so.

The fairies all set sail in eggshells across the sea. The ones from the parish of Sourin were crossing the Westray Firth to Westray when their eggshell boats sank, and they were all drowned. From that day forward there have been no fairies seen in Rousay.

How Tam Scott Lost His Sight

Tam Scott was as good a seaman as ever walked a deck or pulled an oar, that was before he lost his sight of course. God knows that there is many a foul heart under a fair face, and Tam found that out to his cost. I'll tell you the tale of how Tam lost his sight. You might learn from it.

Tam was enjoying the Lammas Fair in Kirkwall. He had taken a number of folk over from Sanday in his parly boat[1], and now his time was his own. Tam was walking up and down through the fair, when he met a tall dark man. "The top of the day to you," said the stranger, "As much to you," said Tam, "but I'm a liar if I know who speaks to me." "Never heed!" said the man, "Will you take a cow of mine to one of the north isles? I'll pay double freight for taking you so soon from the fair." "That will I," said Tam, as he thought that it was too good a deal to miss.

Tam ran to look for Willie o' Gorn, the man who worked on the boat with him. Tam found Willie lying at the head of the Anchor Close, dead drunk. Tam gave him a little kick, and a big oath, then ran to the shore. He got the boat ready by himself, just in time to see the dark stranger coming leading the cow. When the man came to the shore he lifted the cow up in his arms like it was a sheep, and set it in the boat. Tam stared in amazement. "By my soul, good man, you were not behind when strength was handed out."

When they got under way, Tam said "Where are we to steer for?" "East of Shapinsay," said the man. When they reached Shapinsay, Tam said "Where now?" "East of Stronsay," said the man. When they were off Mill Bay in Stronsay, Tam said: "You'll be for landing here?" "East of

---

[1] *An old type of sailing boat.*

Sanday." came the reply. Now Tam liked a crack and he tried his best to get a blether with the man, but he was not one for talking. "A close tongue keeps a safe head," he would gruffly say, and nothing more.

Tam looked at his strange passenger, and he started to think that he was not quite what he seemed. As they sailed along through the east sea Tam saw a bank of fog rising before them. Tam said: "I'm afraid it's coming mist." The man only replied: "A close tongue keeps a safe head!" Tam said: "That may be true, but a close mist wouldn't be very safe for you and me." The stranger smiled a sulky smile, it was the first smile that Tam had seen on his dour face.

By this time the fog had lit up, like a cloud with the setting sun shining on it. Then the fog began to lift as quickly as it had fallen, and Tam saw a beautiful little island in front of them. On that fair land were men and women walking around, cattle grazing and fields of yellow corn swaying in the breeze. As Tam stared in wonder at the scene the man sprang towards him, saying: "I must blindfold you for a little while. Do what you're told and no ill shall befall you." Tam remembered the man lifting the cow so easily, and thought it wise to go along with him, so he was blindfolded with his own napkin.

After a few minutes Tam felt the boat grind on a gravelly shore. He heard many voices as people talked to his strange passenger. He also heard the most lovely music, the most beautiful that ever lighted on mortal ears. It was the song of the mermaids who were sitting on the shore, each hoping for a human husband. Tam could see them from the corner of his right eye, as it was not covered by the napkin. The beautiful maidens and their lovely singing nearly put Tam out of his wits with joy. Then he heard the man shout: "You idle limmers, you need not think to win this man with your singing! He has a wife and bairns of his own in Sanday Isle." With that the music changed to a sad lament that nearly broke Tam's heart, and brought tears to his eyes.

The cow was lifted from the boat, and a bag of money placed at Tam's feet in the stern. The boat was then cast off from the shore, but the black-hearted wretches of Fin men turned the boat against the sun. As they pushed off the boat one of them shouted: "Keep the oustrom[2] end of the fore thaft bearing on the Brae of Warsetter, and you'll soon make land." As the boat sailed away, Tam tore the blindfold off, but he was once more surrounded by the thick fog. He soon sailed out of the mist and found himself back in bright sunshine with not a cloud in the sky. Behind him lay the mist like a thick curtain. He saw another sight that he liked better, for there was the Brae of Warsetter just as the Fin man had said.

As Tam sailed his boat home he opened the bag of money. He found that he had been well paid, but all the coins were coppers. The Fin Folk like the white money too well to part with any silver.

The next year Tam went to the Lammas Fair as usual. Later he would often wish that he had stayed in his bed that day, but wishing did Tam no good for by then it was too late. Tam walked up and down the fair as usual, talking to old friends, and taking a cog of ale with them. Then who should Tam see but his strange, dark-featured passenger that he

---

[2] *Starboard, (right).*

had ferried the previous year. Tam ran up to the man with a smile and said: "How is all with you, good man? So might I thrive, as I am glad to see you! Come and take a cog of ale with me. And how have you been since last I saw you?" "Did you ever see me?" asked the man, and an ugly look passed over his dark face. As he spoke he took out what Tam thought was a snuff box, opened the lid, then blew some of the stuff that was in it straight into Tam's eyes, saying: "You shall never have to say that you saw me again." And from that moment on poor Tam never saw another blink of sweet light on his two eyes. You see, you should not be too friendly towards people that you don't know.

The Rousay Changeling

There was once a woman in Rousay who had a baby. It was a bonnie healthy bairn, and was the apple of the proud parents' eyes. But then it began to change. It grew weak and started to waste away and pine. The mother was very worried, and called for help from a wise woman who lived in the district. The wise woman came to see the bairn and took a good long look at it. The mother pressed her to find out what ailed the bairn, she was at her wits end with worry.

The wise woman said that her bairn had been taken by the fairies and they had left one of their own in its place as a changeling. She told the mother that if she wanted to have her child restored to her she must go to a rock face called the Hammers of the Sinians. It was up the hill past Muckle Water. She must take with her a wedge of steel and a bible. There she would find a cleft in the rock at a certain place, and she had to drive the steel wedge into the crack. The rock would then open and she would see a woman sitting with her bairn on her knee. She must not say a word, but strike the fairy woman three times on the face with the bible. She must then turn around, without uttering a sound, and return home.

The mother took steel and a bible and headed up the hill to the rock face. She found the cleft in the rock as she had been told by the wise woman, and drove in the steel wedge. The rock opened and there was the fairy woman, sitting with the bairn on her knee. The fairy woman tried everything she could to make the woman speak, but to no avail. The woman remembered what the wise woman had said, and held her tongue. She raised the bible and struck the fairy three times on the face then she left. She went home at a brisk speed, hope and fear burning in her breast. When she arrived at her house, there was the baby back before her, as fat and healthy as when it was taken.

The City at the Bottom of the Sea

One fine evening, after the harvest was gathered home for the winter, Arthur Dearness took his pail and went to gather limpets for bait. Arthur was a big, strong, good-looking man and was well liked in his native island of Sanday. No one could beat him at trials of strength. He could throw the big hammer or putting-stone much farther than anyone else. His home was called Corsdale, and he was soon to take home a wife. She was Clara Peace, the laird of Norse Skeel's daughter, and they were to be married a month after Hallomass.[1]

Arthur went to the outer point of Hamaness for the limpets, as he knew it was a good place for them. As he picked them from the rocks, he noticed a group of large ones stuck to the top side of a shelf of rock that hung out over the sea. To get at the limpets he had to lie flat on his front with his head and arms hanging over the edge. He raised his pick to strike off a limpet when he heard a strange sound. A beautiful music hung in the air all around him, sending his head in a spin. He did not have the power to say "God save me". for he could move neither lip nor limb. The sweet music grew louder and louder, until Arthur saw a face far beneath him under the sea. It was the most beautiful face that Arthur had ever seen, a woman more lovely than any that he had set eyes on before. Suddenly two milk-white arms were around his neck and Arthur was pulled down into the sea. His head spun like he was drunk, and then everything went dark.

When Arthur woke he found himself sitting in the bow of a boat. The boat was gliding over the sea as fast as an arrow through the air. In the stern of the boat sat the most beautiful creature that Arthur had ever

---

[1] *The first week of November.*

seen. It was a woman, but Arthur had never seen such a lovely face in all his born days. Her hair shone like spun gold and her blue eyes sparkled with a beauty beyond words. She was naked from the waist up and her snow white skin could be seen between the tresses of her long yellow hair that flowed down over her shoulders. Her lower half was covered by a silvery skirt that shone like the moon on a frosty winter's night. The end of this skirt hung over the stern of the boat and was twisted into the shape of a tail. With this tail she propelled the boat. Under this skirt Arthur could see two pearly white feet resting on the bottom of the boat. Arthur saw that the boat was flying over the waves towards the setting sun, and not a stone of Orkney was to be seen. He knew that he had been carried off by a mermaid, and a great longing came over him to see his home and Clara once more. It came into his mind to say a prayer, but he could not remember the words. At that moment the mermaid sprang forward to the bow of the boat. She threw her arms about his neck, kissed him, and breathed into his mouth. Her breath went down his throat like honey, and he forgot all about home and Clara. Instead all he could think about was the lovely creature that sat in front of him. Arthur fell deeply in love with the mermaid.

The mermaid sat down next to Arthur in the bow, and he wrapped his arms around her. All the time she was looking up at the sky until she saw a certain star. Arthur could not see it, but mermaids have wonderful eyesight. When they were right under that star she cried out:

"Sea, sea, open to me!
Open the door to Auga."

That was when Arthur first heard the mermaid's name, Auga. As her words rang out in the evening air, the boat, the mermaid and Arthur sank into the deep sea. Arthur found to his amazement that he could breathe under the sea like a fish.

When they came to the bottom of the sea they found themselves in the middle of a great town. Auga led Arthur into a grand palace. In the entrance hall he saw the women servants at work, grinding pearls between quernstones. They came to a room called the silver chamber, and here Auga left him. When she returned Arthur thought that he looked on the noonday sun, for her beauty shone so brightly. Gone was her fish's tail, for now she stood before him in the lovely form of a woman. No mortal woman was so fair as Auga, and Arthur's heart swelled with love. She wore a robe that glittered with gold and silver, but was made dim by the glow of her golden hair. A string of pearls hung around her neck, and every pearl was as big as a cockle shell. She wore no other gems, as no diamond could shine beneath the sparkle of her eyes. Her eyes were deep blue like a cloudless sky on a summer's day, and her love for Arthur shone through them like the sun.

Arthur and Auga sat talking and hugging in the silver chamber. She told him that they were in the great town of Finfolkaheem. That they were to be married, and he was to be forever true to her, and she to him. After he had lived there for three years he would be made a burgher of the town and would rise to great honour. And she said, "You must prepare for the great foy[2] which my folk are making ready to welcome you here." She took out her golden comb, and began to comb her long hair. As she combed she kissed Arthur's face, until his love for her flowed through him like a river.

Auga rose and went over to a large chest and brought out a long silken robe that covered Arthur from shoulder to feet. Then two of her maids entered the room and took off Arthur's rivlins[3] and stockings and then washed his feet. He was told that he must enter the great foy-hall in bare feet, as was the custom. The maids anointed his feet with a sticky ointment, and sprinkled them with pearl dust. They were then ready to go to the foy-hall, and Auga's maids led the way.

Arthur had never seen such a lovely place in his life. The walls, pillars, roof and floor were all made from crystal and everything shone with a strange phosphorescent glow. The hall was full of Fin men and mermaids, and as Auga and Arthur entered they all arose and gave a mighty shout of triumph and welcome. They were led to the high seat, and all the great people of Finfolkaheem sat on either side of them.

All the mermaids came up to where Arthur sat and each one kissed his feet. Mermaids like to kiss human flesh, but they could not kiss his

[2] *A party or celebration.*
[3] *A type of shoe made from untanned hide.*

lips as Auga would not let them. Arthur thought that they were all very beautiful, but none of them was as lovely as his Auga, her eyes outshone them all.

They then started the feast and the tables were laid with all the best produce of the undersea people. There were big troughs heaped up with whale meat, roasted and boiled, and stewed in whale blubber. There were small troughs containing roast and boiled seals and otters. There were big tubs of whale and seal soup, thickened with the roes of cod. There were small dishes of all kinds of fish, chapped heads, and little cakes made from fish liver, called livery foals. There was no bread of any kind, and no vegetables, only sea-weed boiled in oil or stewed in seal fat. Arthur thought that it was all very good, much better than he was used to. Mermaids filled horns with ale and quaichs with blood red wine, and they were never allowed to run dry.

A great dish was then set in front of Auga and Arthur by an old Fin man with a great beard that hung down to his waist. On the dish was a big roasted emmer goose[4]. The old man cut the goose down the middle, lengthways, into two equal parts. "Now bairns," said the old man, "there is a half for each of you. And each of you must eat every morsel of the half; must pick the bones bare. The bones will be counted when you are done, to see that each one has eaten the whole. For this is the true sign of marriage among the Fin Folk. So beware, both, not to leave one morsel of your half, for on this depends your luck."

While Arthur was eating his half of the goose, he felt something sitting on his knee. He saw that it was a black cat. He was also aware that no one else could see the cat. As Auga picked the wing bone of her goose the cat took the half of the wedding bone from Auga's plate, picked it clean, and left it on the plate. As Arthur picked his wing the cat seized the goose's leg, picked the bones, and left them on the table. Arthur was glad of the help, as he thought that his stomach would burst, but he did not want to be beaten by Auga.

Arthur did not know what good the cat had done him, for by eating his part of the half it had broken a dangerous charm. When the goose was eaten, stoop and roop, the old man with the long beard counted

---

[4] *Great Northern Diver.*

the bones of each half, and found them equal. He then set a great horn mounted with silver and pearls between them. It was filled with blood red wine, and the smell of it made Arthur's head spin with delight. The old man said: "This is your wedding horn, drink it fair between you both, and it makes you two one for ever and aye. And Trow[5] crack the jaw of the one that drinks unfair!"

Auga raised the horn to her lips and drank with a right good will. It was then passed to Arthur who raised it to his lips with great glee. But every time he tried to take a drink, the same cat knocked its head against the bottom of the horn so that the most of the wine ran down Arthur's front between his robe and skin. Arthur was annoyed about this, as the wine was so good, but it was not in his power to hinder the cat.

When the wedding horn was dry the young maidens carried Auga to one end of the hall and laid her on a rug. The young men carried Arthur to the other end of the hall and laid him on another rug. Both were then rolled to and fro on the rug. This was to done to aid digestion, and to hinder any bad effects of such a heavy meal.

After they had been rolled for a time they were brought into the dancing hall. If Arthur thought the foy-hall beautiful, then the dancing hall was even lovelier. Its walls were hung with curtains that were the colour of the merry dancers[6] when they shine at their brightest on a clear frosty night. They were kept in gentle motion like the real merry dancers, shimmering and changing colour all the time. This trick was done with the help of the Fin Folk's magic. The dancing went on for long, and every dancer was barefoot. Arthur thought that it was the most lovely sight to see the milk white feet of the mermaids tripping out from under their embroidered skirts. Arthur danced like there was no tomorrow, and the ale cog was seldom from his head.

When all the dancers were weary they sat down on the floor, and a big tub was brought around. The tub was full of what they called "good night drink", and everyone filled their drinking horns. Then they all sang "The Fin Folk's Foy Song", a strange song, for all the lines ended in the same rhyme. As they sang the last word they gave a shout as loud

[5] *The Devil.*
[6] *The aurora borealis.*

as a clap of thunder. Arthur thought that the roof would split.

Two stately maidens took up Auga and carried her from the hall on the "King's cushion". Six maidens went before her, and five followed. After a while a horn sounded and two Fin men bore Arthur away, six men going in front, and five behind. He was carried into a golden chamber, where he saw Auga lying in bed. The young Fin men undressed Arthur and lay him in bed beside Auga. The thirteen young men and thirteen young women then danced around the bed before leaving.

Arthur was very drunk by this time, yet he was sure that he could see the black cat sitting at the foot of the bed. The cat dived under the blankets. Arthur could feel it lying between him and Auga, but its shape had changed for now it was a great eel. When Arthur tried to put his hand over to Auga, the eel would bite it. He cursed this cat and eel, but he was powerless to do anything. He thought that he could hear the eel whispering sweet nothings into Auga's ear and with that he fell asleep.

Auga and Arthur rose at rising time, there was no day or night in Finfolkaheem. They had a hearty breakfast and then they kissed lovingly for a while. Arthur went out hunting with the Fin men. They rode on sea-horses and hunted all the wild animals in the sea. When they were tired of the chase they returned home and feasted. This went on for some days, Arthur was not sure how long. He saw all around the beautiful town of Finfolkaheem, it was a wonder to behold. There were a great many houses with lovely gardens where different coloured seaweed grew in place of flowers. The Fin Folk had large flocks of whales, sea-cows and seahorses, all quite tame. At the blowing of a horn the herds drove the flocks to town where the mermaids milked the whales and sea-cows. The Fin Folk are very fond of whale milk. Arthur thought it was great sport to hunt with the Fin Folk. They hunted on sea-horses, and used otters and seals as dogs. When Arthur returned from the hunt Auga would be waiting for him with a loving kiss. She would wash his feet and comb his hair, and he was always given the very best of food. Arthur was as happy as the day was long, and the days were long enough in Finfolkaheem. He never once thought of home, or Clara who was weeping for him. Auga's spell was too strong, and Arthur and the mermaid were very much in love.

Now when Arthur had disappeared all his family and friends had searched the shore. For many days they looked, but they found nothing. On the evening of the day that Arthur vanished, Clara was told the news. She sank into her chair and said nothing. Her grief was so strong that words, even tears failed her. Her parents sent for her Aunt Marion. Aunt Marion was the goodwife of Grindaley, and was a spae-wife. She was well known for her wisdom and skill at curing the illnesses of both the body and mind. She had more wit than her own, but she never used it for harm, only good.

As soon as Marion got the news, she sent the messenger back to Norse

Skeel with a reply. She would be with them in the morning, but to keep up a good heart in the meantime. She then locked herself away in her little chamber and what she did I do not know. She stayed there until past the middle hours of the night. When she came out she was covered with sweat, like she had been working hard all night. In the morning she rode to Norse Skeel, stopping at Corsdale on the way. She told Arthur's family to cheer up, saying: "Your son's a living man, and if all goes fair, you'll see him yet." But the folk shook their heads, saying: "The goodwife of Grindaley is wrong this time, anyway."

On she rode to Norse Skeel, where she tried to cheer up Clara, but with little luck. Clara was sorely hurt at the loss of her sweetheart. Three weeks passed, and not a sight of Arthur was to be seen. Everyone had given him up for lost, his body was not even cast ashore. All the people mourned for Arthur. because he was well liked by all who knew him, but Clara mourned most of all.

Now I must tell you about Arthur and what had become of him. One day Arthur and Auga sat in her chamber, lovingly embracing. She sat on his knee, her arms around his waist and her head on his breast. He sat with his left arm around her neck, his left hand on her bosom. With his right hand he patted and stroked her long yellow hair. Auga looked lovingly into his face, her eyes were the most beautiful thing that Arthur had ever seen. They smiled at each other, Arthur was deep under her spell. The mermaid's spell is very strong and Arthur would have now been hopelessly lost, if it had not been for the black cat.

Unseen by Auga, the black cat sat on Arthur's left shoulder watching every movement. As Arthur stroked her hair with his right hand the cat made a grab for it. It seized his forefinger between its two forepaws and quickly drew a cross with Arthur's finger on Auga's brow. Auga gave a piercing shriek, there was a noise louder than the loudest thunder. then the sight went from Arthur's eyes and he fell senseless to the floor.

How long he lay there he did not know, but when Arthur came to his senses he was lying on the rocks at Hamaness, at the same spot where he had been picking limpets. Above him stood the figure of a woman, it was Aunt Marion, the goodwife of Grindaley. She helped Arthur to his feet, he looked at her and said: "The Best be thanked for you and your black cat! But for you both, I should have been a prisoner all my life in Finfolkaheem." The old spae-wife brought him home and all his love for Clara returned stronger than ever. They were married next Martinmas[7] and lived in joy for many years.

The old folk used to say that they had often heard in the mirk of the morning Auga sing a sad song on the rocks of Hamaness. Maybe she sings there to this day.

[7] *November 11.*

The Selkie Man

Jessie lived with her father on the island of Sanday. He was employed in the shipping of peats from the neighbouring island of Eday. Sanday has no peat of its own, so fuel had to be imported from outside, unless you used dried tangles[1] and cow scones[2].

One day her father left on the morning tide to sail to Eday for another load of peats. The weather grew worse and worse as the day went on, and he was forced to spend the night there. Jessie sat alone in the house that night, waiting for her father's return. All of a sudden there was a banging at the door. She jumped from her seat and went to see who was there. To her surprise it was a stranger who was at the door. He asked if he might come in to shelter from the wind and rain, for it was a wild night. Jessie told him that he'd better leave, as she was alone and it would not be right for him to sit in the house when her father was not at home. The man pleaded for her to have mercy on a poor stranger on such a cold rainy night as this. He offered to pay for his night's lodgings, and as she knew that they could use the money she agreed to let him in.

She showed him to the peat fire that burned in the middle of the room, and told him to sit there and dry his wet clothes. To her surprise the stranger said that the fire was too hot for his liking. and he sat in a corner of the room. He was a dark, handsome man, and Jessie wondered who he was and what business had brought him to Sanday. She also wondered why he wanted a place to stay at all, as he sat in the shadows still in his wet clothes.

[1] *Seaweed.*
[2] *Cow dung.*

The stranger that Jessie had let in was not a man at all, but one of the selkie folk. Selkie men are fond of human lasses and are always on the lookout for any opportunity. What happened that night is not for us to know, but nine months later Jessie was delivered of a healthy baby boy. But he was no ordinary boy, for he was half bairn and half selkie. For half the moon's course he lived at home on the island with his mother. For the other half he donned his flippers and whiskers and lived in the sea with his father and his selkie family.

Tam Bichan and the Trow

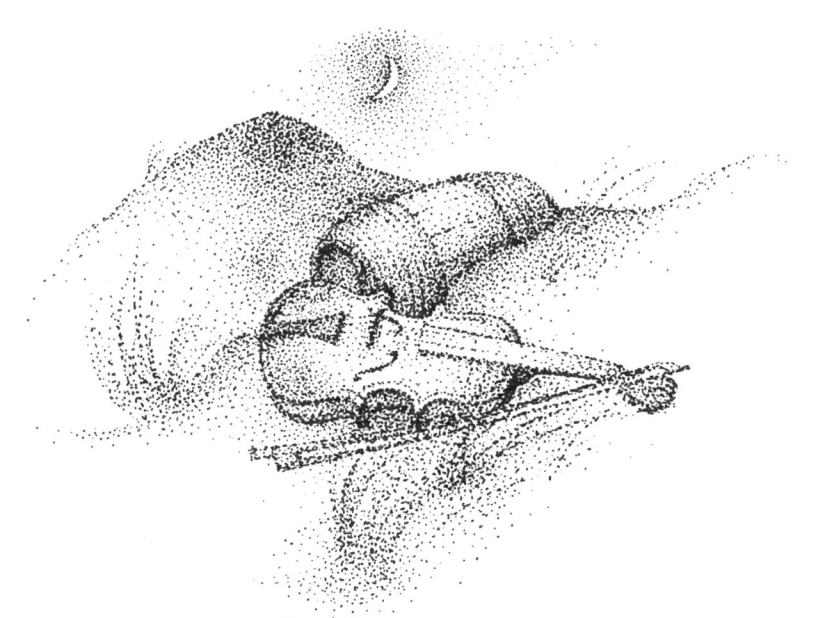

am Bichan was a bright, cheery soul who liked nothing better than to play the fiddle. His playing was famous all over the East Mainland, and much in demand in his native Deerness. Whenever there was a wedding or a muckle supper[1], Tam the fiddler was always the first to be asked.

It happened one Johnsmas Eve that Tam took a walk by the beach at Taracliff Bay. That thin strip of sand is all that holds Deerness to the rest of the Mainland. As was his custom, Tam carried his fiddle with him. Now as every fool knows, or may find to his cost, midsummer and

[1] *Harvest Home.*

midwinter are the times that the trows have the most power over mortal man. It is then that they roam the earth, looking for bairns, mothers or cattle to steal away to their own lands. Not only that, but the beach, or rather the strip between high and low water, is the domain of the Devil and all his subjects.

Tam soon found that he was not alone. A peedie[2] man dressed in grey was walking towards him. He had a long grey beard and his dark eyes glinted with a mischievous light. The peedie man greeted Tam in a polite manner and invited him back to his place to play the fiddle for him and a few friends. Tam thanked him, and said he would gladly play for him. So Tam set off with his host, and the peedie man led the way.

Tam followed his companion right up the the great mound of Dingieshowe. Much to Tam's surprise there was a door standing open in the side of the knowe. They both entered and were soon walking down a long, steep tunnel. It was dark, and Tam wondered if he was doing the right thing, for he knew that his host must be a trow. Down and down they went, on and on right to the heart of the knowe. At last Tam found himself in a huge room.

The trow pointed to a large cask that was standing on the floor and told him he might sit there. Tam dutifully perched himself on the barrel while the trow pulled the spigot from it, and out flowed the most delicious smelling ale. The trow gave a cog of it to Tam, saying that it was heather ale and Tam would not have tasted the like of it before. It was by far the best drop of drink that Tam had ever tasted.

The ale put life in him, and he was soon playing the fiddle like a demon. His fingers flew over the strings as if they had a life of their own. Tam had never played better than he did that night. As the night's entertainment came to an end, so did the ale in the cask. As the last of it slipped down Tam's throat he smiled a contented smile. He thanked his host for a most enjoyable evening, and started on his journey to the upper world.

Tam found himself back outside the mound of Dingieshowe, but there was no longer any sign of the door. He shook his head, which was still reeling from the heather ale, and took a deep breath of the cold morning

[2] *Small, little.*

air. Thinking of home and bed, he started to walk to his house. It was then that Tam started to notice things. He was not sure what it was, but things seemed somehow different.

When he reached his home Tam could not believe his eyes. The house was a ruin with no roof. His mother was nowhere to be seen either. The shock was almost too much for him, and he wandered off in a stupor. At last he met a boy walking on the road. He stopped him and asked what had happened to the house and the old woman who lived there. The boy said that he had better come with him to his father's house, for he did not know the answers to Tam's questions.

Tam followed the boy to his house. There he found an older man sitting at a table, eating his breakfast. There was something familiar about the man's face, but Tam couldn't place it. When the man looked up and saw Tam his face went as white as a sheet. "Tam Bichan, is that you? No, it can't be." said the man. "Aye, I'm Tam Bichan, but who are you?" The man stared at him, and his eyes glowed in his head like a burning peat. "I'm Andrew Delday, don't you remember me?" Tam's head reeled. He knew Andrew Delday all right, but he was a much younger man, about the same age as himself. How could this be him, he was much too old.

After Tam had composed himself Andrew told him the whole story. Someone had seen Tam heading towards Taracliff Bay with his fiddle, but he never returned. People thought that he had fallen over the cliffs and his body carried out to sea. All this had taken place some fourteen years and a day before. His mother had died, and the house was never re-let. Tam could not believe his ears. He thought that he had spent just one night with the trow in Dingieshowe.

The news of the fiddler's return spread like wildfire around the parish. Yes, Tam Bichan was back, and he didn't look a day older then he had done when he went missing. Old Andrew Delday declared that "the very cap on his head was the same." Tam was the only one who did not wish to talk about his miraculous return. He did tell one of his friends that he had seen the hilltrows and Fin Folk. He said that the Fins were the only ones that seemed to be male and female. They were wide between the eyes, and had skin as soft as a cat. They had left their homes under the waves to join in the dancing, and they clappered in rivlins[3] on the floor.

Tam was urged to find himself a wife, but he shunned company, especially female. A skillie[4] wife was found to keep house for him, but he had little to say to her. He was loath to play the fiddle, though he was often asked. It was said that now and again he was heard to thumb strange tunes when he thought he was alone.

One day he was seen to wander off in the direction of the shore with his fiddle. This time he never returned, and that is all that I can tell you about Tam Bichan the fiddler.

[3] *A type of shoe made from untanned hide.*
[4] *Skilful, in this case a housekeeper.*

The Giants of Hoy

On the island of Hoy is a strange stone, hollowed out to form a chamber. It was said to have been made by a giant for himself and his pregnant wife. There is a stone bed inside the chamber with a stone pillow, and a depression at one side for the wife's swollen belly. Their fine hall is still to be seen, and bears the name "The Dwarfie Stane". As the name suggests it is not a huge dwelling for a giant, yet alone two of them.

The giant and his wife were not alone in Hoy though, oh no! There was also another giant who hated his neighbour and his wife to the point of murder. He thought that if he killed the other two he alone would be master of all of Hoy. He could also take possession of the fine hall that his rival had made. The stone hall had but one doorway in its side. The evil giant took a stone and shaped it so that it fitted the opening exactly.

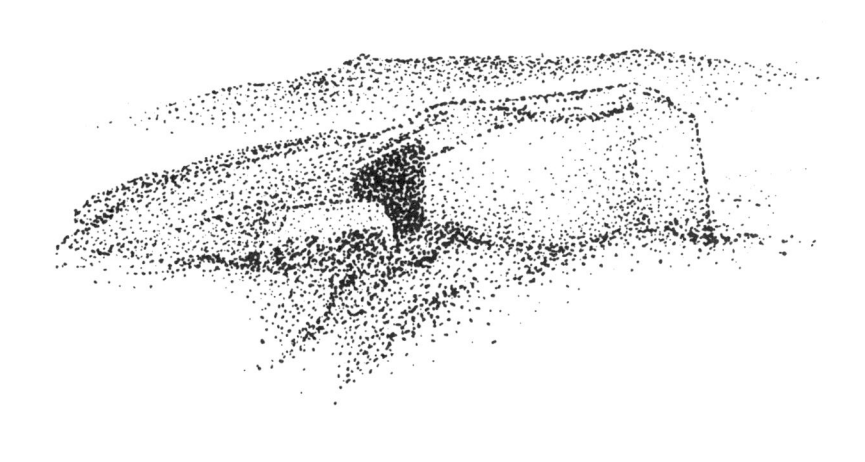

He climbed to the top of the highest hill, and waited till his victims were in bed. When he was happy that they were snugly tucked in, he fitted the stone in his sling. He swung it around his head and flung it with all his might at the door of the hall. His aim was straight and true and the stone struck the doorway, filling it completely.

The noise woke the sleeping giant inside, who tried to force the stone out of the door. After he saw that this would not work he took his hammer and began to strike the ceiling of the hall. He hammered and hammered until he broke a hole right through the roof. He climbed out and ran after the other giant in a great rage. And if he did not catch him, they might be running yet.

The Shetland Fin Wife

The goodman of Faracleat in Rousay was a successful trader who used to make regular trips to Norway. As he returned from his third voyage one year his ship was caught in a gale, and driven onto the rocks of Shetland. The goodman and the ship's crew managed to struggle ashore alive, but they had lost everything. Autumn was quickly giving way to winter. Strong winds and heavy seas would make sure that the Orkneymen would not be able to return home for the rest of that year.

The goodman of Faracleat took lodgings with an old woman who was good to him and treated him well. Now the year wore on and the winds still howled with rage around the little house. It was Christmas Eve, and the goodman sat staring into the fire with a heavy heart. He was not interested in the food that the old woman offered him, and he had little to say to her. The old woman tried to cheer him up and urged him to eat, but with no luck. At last he spoke of what was troubling him, "Alack-a-day! How can I be merry this night? Tomorrow is Yuleday. Oh, dear! It'll be the first Yuleday that I have been away from my own fireside, and from my wife and bairns since I was married. Alas! well may I be sad and dour'"

"Well," said the old woman, "I warrant you would fain be beside your own folk at such a time. And I'm well sure you would give the best cow in your byre if you could be beside your wife by cock crow on Yule morning." "Aye! That I would, with all my heart, Lord knows!" "Well, well! It's all well that ends well," said the old woman, "but take yourself a drop of gin, and go to bed, goodman, and if you tell me your dreams in the morning, I'll give you a silver mark for hansel[1] on

---

[1] *A gift given during celebrations.*

Yuleday." So the man took a drink and went to bed and slept soundly until morning.

The goodwife of Faracleat lay in her lonely bed and thought about her husband. Was he still alive, and if so, where was he? She thought that it would be a sad Yule in the house of Faracleat that year. She rolled over and went to sleep, but was woken in the morning by the feeling that someone was in the bed beside her. As she came to her senses she could hear the low snoring of a man under the blankets next to her. She fetched the intruder a mighty wallop with her fists, and cried out in rage: "You ill-bred, ill-descended villain! How dare you come into an honest wife's bed. Get out, you great beast, or, by the Lord who made you, I'll tear you to rags!" "Is that your voice, my own Maggie?" said the man, as she grabbed him by the throat. When she heard his voice she let go her grip and said: "Bless me! Are you my own goodman?" And so it was. He had been transported from Shetland to Rousay by the magic of the old woman, for you see she was not just any old woman, but a Fin Wife. Their magic is much stronger than anything that mankind can command.

As the goodwife hugged her goodman a thought occurred to him, and he said: "Goodwife, I doubt you'll not be so glad when you come to know what it cost to take me home!" And they both dressed, and went into the byre. Sure enough, their best cow was gone! The goodwife cried out: "Oh! it's Brenda! She's taken the best cow, and the best milker in the byre!"

And that is as true as I'm sitting here this night, for a man called Johnie Flett from Rousay was in Shetland the following summer and what should he see tethered outside the old woman's house but Brenda the cow! He knew the cow well, and he swore that that was her he saw chewing the cud in Shetland.

The Hogboon of Hellihowe

In the north end of the parish of Burness in Sanday is the house of Hellihowe. Near to the house was a mound where the hogboon lived. As long as the hogboon received his share of the croft's produce all was well, for he brought good luck to the place. One day the man of the house brought home his new wife. She knew nothing of the hogboon, and never poured so much as a drop of milk or ale over the mound. She also scraped clean all the pots before they were put away, so the hogboon got nothing.

This state of affairs did not please the hogboon one little bit. The luck of the farm soon turned sour as the hogboon took out his spite on the hapless couple. Things started to disappear, just when they were most needed, and the poor crofter and his wife were the victims of the most outrageous practical jokes. This went on for some time until the poor couple were driven to despair.

At last it was decided that they would ask the laird if they could move house. The man set off to the big house, and was soon back with a bright smile on his face. They were given the lease of another place at the opposite end of the island. One fine summer's morning they set out with a string of ponies carrying all their worldly goods tied to klibbers[1] on their backs. The goodman of the house led the foremost pony which was carrying a kirn. The farther they went from their old home the happier the man was. After some time they drew near to their new house, the man felt like dancing with joy. But all of a sudden the lid of the kirn flew off and the hogboon popped his head out and said: "We're getting a fine day to flit on, goodman".

[1] *A wooden pack saddle.*

The Everlasting Battle

A proclamation was sent far and wide announcing that there was to be a gathering of kings. King Hogni left with a body of men and they sailed in their dragon ships to the assembly. While he was there news was brought to him that King Hedinn had attacked his land and carried off his daughter Hildr. He gathered together an army and sailed after Hedinn with many a curse on his lips.

It was rumoured that Hedinn had travelled north to Norway, so Hogni turned his keel to the north lands. When he arrived in Norway he was told that Hedinn had sailed west to Orkney. Hogni wasted no time and soon he was in full pursuit of his enemy. He found Hedinn on the island of Hoy where he had landed with his army. Hildr went alone to her father with a message from Hedinn. She said he wanted to make peace with him, and he offered Hogni a valuable necklace if he would accept his terms. If he did not accept he would fight, and Hogni and his men could expect no mercy. Hogni was furious when he heard this threat and sent his daughter back to Hedinn with angry words. Hildr returned to Hedinn and told him to prepare for battle.

Both kings moved their armies to the island for the coming fight. Again King Hedinn sued for peace, offering King Hogni much gold if he would be reconciled to him. Hogni refused, saying: "This offer comes too late, if it is peace that thou seekest, for I have already drawn Danisleaf which was fashioned by the dwarves, and every time it is unsheathed a man must die; nor does it ever make a false stroke, and if a man be but pricked by it his wounds may not be mended." Hedinn replied: "Thy boast is merely in thy weapon, not in the end of this encounter; I call any sword trusty which faithfully defends its lord." Both armies clashed together with great fury. The battle raged all that day and it was called the Strife of the Hjadnings. In the evening the kings returned to their ships with their men to prepare for the following day's conflict.

When night fell over the island of Hoy, Hildr visited all the slain on the battlefield. She wove her magic spell over the lifeless bodies and gave them breath once more. Day after day the fight went on, and everyone who was killed was turned to stone. The weapons that were left on the field were also turned to stone as soon as the sun set behind the hills. Dawn brought all the fallen warriors back from the dead, and they rose and took up their weapons once more. Both warriors and weapons are renewed every day, and the battle will go on until the Weird of the Gods, when they will be defeated at the battle of Ragnarok.

Lady Odivere

In Norway lived a lady who's wealth was only outmatched by her great beauty. She lived in a grand castle, and had everything she could wish for. But this lady also had something that she did not want; men. They came from far, they came from near, and they all wanted her hand in marriage, not to mention her fortune. Men came from over the seas in ships, from over the land on fine horses, but the lady treated them with disgust. "Go home and mend the clothes that you have worn out on your journey," she would say. Many a man had to turn for home with a heavy heart, for the lady sent them packing with a frown.

A brave knight called Odivere heard about the beautiful lady and declared that she would be his wife. He was a man who was fond of swordplay, song, and the lasses too. But he was a stubborn man, and liked to get his own way. He fell on his knees and swore the Odin oath that he would make her his bride. To swear an oath by him that hung on the tree is a dangerous thing, for Odin is a fickle friend.

Odivere set out to the lady's palace to woo her. The lady looked on him with favour, and they spent much time in each other's company. Time wore on, and the lady fell for Odivere's charm. They were married, and a grand wedding it was. Odivere was a boastful man, and he bragged that he had won his wife by the Odin oath.

Now Odivere grew tired of living as a married man. He longed for the thrill of battle, and he decided to go to the Holy Land to fight against the pagans. He made ready for the journey; his men were happy to be on the march again. The lady was broken hearted, and she stayed in her room weeping.

Odivere fought long and hard in Guthaland. He grew rich with the plunder he had gathered, and in the evenings his time was spent in song and laughter. He travelled to the great city of Muckle Gerth[1] where he found feasting and drinking at every turn. He also found pretty women to pass an evening with, and his thoughts never turned to his own beautiful wife. He stayed there long, and it was to his liking. He was in no hurry to go back home.

The lady waited with a sore heart. Every day she would comb her golden hair and put on her finery in case Odivere should return. Many an hour she spent on the castle wall looking out over the land, longing for her husband to come back to her, but he never came. No message came to tell her if he was alive or dead, no news at all. Days turned into weeks, months turned to years, and still he did not come.

One evening, after the sun had just set, a mighty knight arrived at the castle. He beat his fist against the gate, shouting out to let him enter. He bellowed out to open the gate for he needed a bed for the night. It was dark, and he had a long way yet to travel. The porter on the gate refused, saying that no stranger could spend the night in the hall

---

[1] *Mikligardr, O.N. "the great city", Byzantium, (Istanbul)*

while the master was over the sea. The knight warned the porter that he would feel the weight of his hand if he did not let him in. He also said to go and get the fair lady who lived there, for he had news of Odivere. The gate was opened and in walked the knight. He was a very big man, and finely dressed. The women in the hall said that they had never seen such a stately knight, and he set many hearts fluttering. He walked up to the Lady Odivere, took off his silk cap and went down on one knee. He placed a golden ring on the lady's lap, saying: "A token from your husband." Her face grew white when she saw it. "I left him well, in good spirits. He is now known as Sir Odivere." said the knight. He told them of Odivere's fame throughout Guthaland, how he had slain many pagans and driven their armies before him.

Now when the lady saw the ring she never listened to a word that the knight had been saying. She held her handkerchief up to her face so that the people there could not see how she had turned white. But her lovely cheeks grew as red as the rose again, and a sparkle came into her eyes. She bade the knight to rise, saying that he had done her good by coming to her hall. She ordered the servants to bring out the best blood-red wine and to set a feast for the knight. The knight was good company, telling stories of battles fought and of fair ladies. He told of Odivere and his honoured place in Guthaland. But he also hinted that Odivere still had an eye for the lasses and was never at a loss for their company.

When the feast was over, and it had grown late, the servants cleared the hall and then went to bed. Lady Odivere and the knight sat alone in the hall, talking. "Why did you bring me back that ring?" asked the lady, "for it brings me pain to see it again. It reminds me of the time when I was in love with you." The knight said, "You know that you were always dear to me. When you gave me the ring on that moonlight night, you swore to be mine forever. I have travelled far over land and sea, but I have never found another woman to love." "Be quiet, be quiet, you false tongued knight, your words spell danger for me. You know what broke us up, it was the Odin oath." He took her hand and led her to the stairs. To her lonely bed chamber he brought her, and there they spent the night.

The knight left in the grey light of dawn, no goodbye, no farewell feast. The lady sat in her room, her heart fit to break. When it was day she wished for night, when it was night she wished it was day. Now it became obvious to all that the lady was with child, and the tongues wagged. She felt alone, more alone than she had ever been before.

Lady Odivere had a son, and a fine strong boy he was. The lady sat and rocked the cradle and sang to her little son.

"Ba loo, ba loo my bonnie bairn
Ba loo lillie, ba loo lay,
Sleep you, my peedie[2] bonnie buddo[3]!
You little kens your mother's way.

Aloor[4]! I do not know your father,
Aloor, aloor, my woeful sin!
I do not ken my bairn's father,
Nor yet the land that he lives in.

Aloor, aloor, called shall I be,
A wicked woman by all men,
That I, a married woman, should have
A bairn to him I do not ken."

Then a voice behind her spoke, "Here I am, your bairn's father, although I'm not your husband sweet." "I know that you're my bairn's father, and I have never loved anyone as much as you. But I have a good husband who's far away."

"I do not care about that man, I hope I never see his face again. I will return in six months time to claim my son. I will pay you your nurse's fee, let it never be said that I did not pay my dues." "But who are you, and where do you live?" asked the lady, with the salt tears brimming in her eyes. "San Imravoe is my name, I can walk on land, and swim in the sea. Among the ranks of the selkie folk I am a mighty king. My home is in Sule Skerry, and all the thousands of selkie folk who live there are

[2] *Small, little.*
[3] *A term of endearment.*
[4] *Alas.*

under me. They are in my willing service and they must do what I say." "But how can you carry our bairn to that cold home over the sea? How will you stop the sea from being our bairn's grave?" "I'll carry him safely, for I need neither ship or boat. We'll arrive at Sule Skerry before the sun is high in the sky." "But how will I know my son from all the other selkies that swim in the sea?" "His paws shall be as black as soot, his body as white as the snow." "But my own goodman is a mighty hunter, what if he should prick or club our bairn when he's in his selkie skin?" "I do not fear that, but I fear this, that the cock crow shall find me still here. But come what may, I will return for my son."

And so saying, he left the Lady Odivere. After six months had passed he returned, bringing with him much gold and silver. He took his son to be his heir and rule over all the selkie folk of Sule Skerry when the time came. The Lady Odivere was overcome with grief and she took the golden chain from around her neck and put it on her little son. The chain had been a wedding gift from Odivere. She begged the selkie king to take her with them, she wanted to live with him as his wife. But the selkie man said that she had had her chance, but had given him up for another. With these words he left her, weeping. Many an hour would the lady spend looking out to sea after that, but there was no sign of her lover, or her child.

Now time passed and Odivere returned. He brought with him a great fortune that he had won by the sword. There was great feasting in the castle, and every day was like a holiday.

They danced, sang and told tales. Then they sat down to eat and drink the night away. Odivere soon grew tired of this lifestyle, he complained that they were getting too fat lying around the table. It was fine for a short time, but now he wanted some sport. It was decided that the next day Odivere and his men should go out otter hunting. The following morning at dawn they all headed to the shore, and hunted there for a while. Suddenly a selkie was seen heading out of a geo, and Odivere killed it with one blow. One of his men said: "I have travelled far, and seen many things, but I have never seen a gold chain around a selkie's neck before." Odivere took the chain, and his face grew black. The selkie's body was brought to the hall and Odivere took the lead, his eyes glowing wildly.

"Come down here, Lady Odivere, and read me this riddle." he bellowed. Lady Odivere came down, wondering what all the noise was about. Then she saw the selkie lying dead on the floor, and the gold chain in Odivere's hand. "Aloor, my bonny bairn, oh, what am I born to see! My curse on the hand of the man that did this foul deed." She tore her hair and wept many tears over the body of her own dead selkie child.

Odivere's rage grew stronger. "Your bairn, you say, it's no bairn of mine! I see that when I was away you have been leading a wicked life."

"You left me alone, to lead a lonely life." cried the poor lady, but Odivere was not listening. He said that he had left her with plenty of worldly goods and a fine hall to live in. He also claimed that he had been faithful to her, though that was a bare faced lie. She whipped the golden chain from his hand and brought it down on the top of his head. Odivere ordered his men to take her away.

The Lady Odivere was locked up in a high tower. There was no window to let in light and she was given meagre meals and cold water to drink. It was decided that the lady was to be burnt at the stake, and no mercy was to be shown to her. She sat in the tower and wept bitter tears; all hope was now lost.

San Imravoe called all the selkies together, and the order was given to swim as fast as they could to Norway. Before them they herded all the whales in the North Sea, right up to the sea next to Odivere's castle. The shout went up, "Whales, whales, in all the bays and voes!" Odivere and his men forgot about the burning which was to take place that day. They all ran to their boats to try and drive the whales ashore. They made enough noise to raise the dead, but without any luck. Not one whale did they catch that day, their only reward was a skinful of sore bones. When Odivere and his men returned to the castle they found all the doors standing wide open. The door to the tower lay on the floor and the lady was nowhere to be found.

Odivere was left an unhappy man. He sat in his hall alone and unloved. He cursed the day that he had taken the Odin oath, for it had brought him no luck. So now the tale is told, but remember, swearing an oath to Odin will bring joy at the beginning, but it always ends in disappointment.

The Trowie Snuff-box

John Spence lived at Millbrig in Birsay about the year 1800. One summer's evening John was out herding cattle in the meadow close to the Klick Mill. He saw an old man sitting on the dyke of the meadows of Owlidens, so he thought he would join him for a bit of a crack. John did not know the man, but they began to talk.

The stranger pulled out his snuff-box and took a pinch. He offered it to John, who took it gladly. He saw that it was a very old snuff-box indeed, made of horn and all chewed at one end. Old John inspected it, then said to the stranger: "Ah, man, you have a very trowie snuff-box," meaning it was of poor quality. As soon as he said the word "trow" the old man vanished in glowing sparks and flames and disappeared over the Moss of Teamora. You see the old man was a trow, or "filtyman" as the old folk sometimes called them, and they can't stand to hear their name mentioned.

When old John had recovered from the shock he looked at the snuff-box that was still in his hand. To his amazement he found that it was nothing more than a lump of dried horse dung.

The Suiter from the Sea

A long time ago there lived an old man and his daughter in the South Parish of South Ronaldsay. The young woman cooked and cleaned and looked after her father, while he worked the small croft. One night the old man went to his bed, barring the house door before he left. The girl sat by the fire for a short while before her thoughts turned to sleep. Suddenly, the latch sprang up and the door opened. A tall, dark man entered the room and sat himself down by the fire. The girl was a bit frightened by him, there was something about him that she didn't like. The man started to talk, and he sat and talked with the girl all night. It was morning before he left.

The girl told her father about the man, and he agreed to sit up with her that night in case he should come back. The old man was sure that it was no human man that was courting his daughter, but a sea man. That evening the old man barred the door, as was his custom, and sat by the fire along with his daughter. After a while the latch sprang up and the door opened. The old man knew that he had barred the door tight shut, so it could only be opened by means of magic. The man entered, and the old man made him welcome. They sat by the fire chatting away for a while, then the old man said: "You know, I'm in an awful predicament, a lot of trouble. and I don't know what to do about it." "Well, said the stranger, "what's wrong?" "I've a fine young cow in the byre, and there's a sea bull taken to come and visit her. No matter what I do, how I tie the byre door, that bull's in with the cow in the morning." "Oh, that's easy put a stop to," said the man, "cut some hair off her tail and some parings off her hoof, put that above the byre door and he won't be able to come in." "Oh, that's very good!" said the old man. "Well, it's time I went to bed." So off he went to bed and the man sat talking to the girl for the rest of the night, only leaving when it was morning.

The next day the old man cut off some of his daughter's hair, pared her nails, and put it above the door. That night he barred the door as usual and went and sat by the fire, waiting. The Fin man returned at his usual time and the latch of the door lifted. This time the sea man could not open the door, no matter how hard he tried. The old man and his daughter heard him saying to himself: "Ey, my. There's many a man done themselves ill with their tongues, and I've done the same." With these last words the sea man returned to his home under the waves. and was never seen by the old man or his daughter again.

The Sandwick Fairies

The house of Pow in Sandwick was a change house, meaning it had a licence to sell ale. People from the surrounding districts used to meet there and wash the day's dust from their throats with a drink of beer. A man from Hestwell had been at Pow and had had a few drinks. On his way home he fell asleep near the Howans of Huntisgarth, which was a well-known fairy haunt. Suddenly, he was awakened by a loud noise. He looked up and saw the brae covered with fairy riders. He got to his feet and ran home as fast as his legs would take him, for he was very frightened by the sight.

He later told the story to an old woman who lived at the house of Aith. She told him that the fairies got neither of what they were after that night. A daughter had been born at the house at the same time as the fairies were at large, and in the daylight they found one of their cows had been nearly strangled in the byre.

The Water Trows

A farmer who lived in the Kirkness district of Sandwick was having a lot of trouble from the water trows who lived in the neigbouring loch. When he was drying corn in his kiln, he would return to find the kiln fire had been put out. The water trows were fond of playing tricks on him too. Things were always found to be broken or hidden when he needed to use them.

After a while it occurred to the farmer to hide in the barn where the kiln was, and see what he could do. When he was next attending his kiln he did not return to his house, but hid under a pile of newly threshed straw. After a short time two water trows came in and sat themselves down by the kiln fire. The farmer tried to get nearer to them, and his motions made the straw move. The one trow saw this and said to his companion, "Straw's moving." His friend replied: "Sit still and warm your belly. Well knows you, straw can't move." After a while the farmer had got quite near to the trows, and he sprang to his feet and threshed them with his flail. The trows ran away, and never troubled him again.

Hilda-land

Annie Norn was a bonnie young lass who lived on the Mainland of Orkney. One evening she went to the shore to fetch some salt water to boil the supper in. In those days salt was expensive, so they used seawater instead. Well, that night Annie never returned. They hunted high and low, but Annie was nowhere to be found. People said that the trows had taken her, and the old folk warned: "Take care of yourselves, bairns, and never go on the ground between the lines of high and low water when the sun is down. God take care of us all!"

Three or four years later an Orkney ship was on her way home from Norway in the autumn of the year. On board was a cousin of Annie Norn, a lad by the name of Willie Norn. Now this ship was caught up in a violent storm, and was tossed around the North Sea for weeks. The crew were exhausted and had no idea where they were, for they could see neither sun nor stars. When the winds fell the crew were no better off, for a thick mist covered the sea. They did not know in what direction they should steer. What was worse was that the wind had fallen completely and only just managed to move the torn sails. They lay becalmed for days; the ship stood still on the water and never moved. The men began to get restless, saying that the ship was bewitched like the one in the story that lay on the sea until all the men died and the ship became a rotting hulk.

As they bemoaned their fate they saw something travelling over the sea towards the ship. It was a small boat rowed by a lone woman. The men thought that she was a Fin wife, and said that they should not let her on board the ship. As they discussed what to do the woman sprang over the railings like a cat and landed on the deck. Willie Norn recognised her as his long lost cousin Annie, saying: "Lord, lass, is that you Annie?" "Oh, aye," said the young woman, "it's me alright. How are the folk at home? Aye boy, if blood had not been thicker than water, you would not have seen me here today." She turned to the crew and said: "You great fools! why are you standing gaping and staring at me as if I were a warlock? Go and veer your vessel about." Annie then put the helm to lee and brought the ship into the wind. She sang out her orders like a born skipper, and the men all jumped to it. When the vessel was got on the other tack she sailed swiftly over the sea with more than her usual speed.

In a short time the men saw what looked like a bright cloud drifting on top of the water. Annie sailed the ship through the cloud and out the other side. The mist had gone, and the tired men found themselves in a land-locked bay. The water was as calm as a millpond with not a ripple on it. On the island they saw beautiful hills and valleys, with many burns babbling down the hillsides, sparkling in the sunshine as they ran through the green valleys. Each bonnie burn sang its own little song as it ran on towards the sea. The skylark took up their song and showered down sweet music from the sunny sky. To the weary storm-tossed mariners it seemed like a haven of bliss. The island was Hilda-Land, the home of the Fin Folk above the waves.

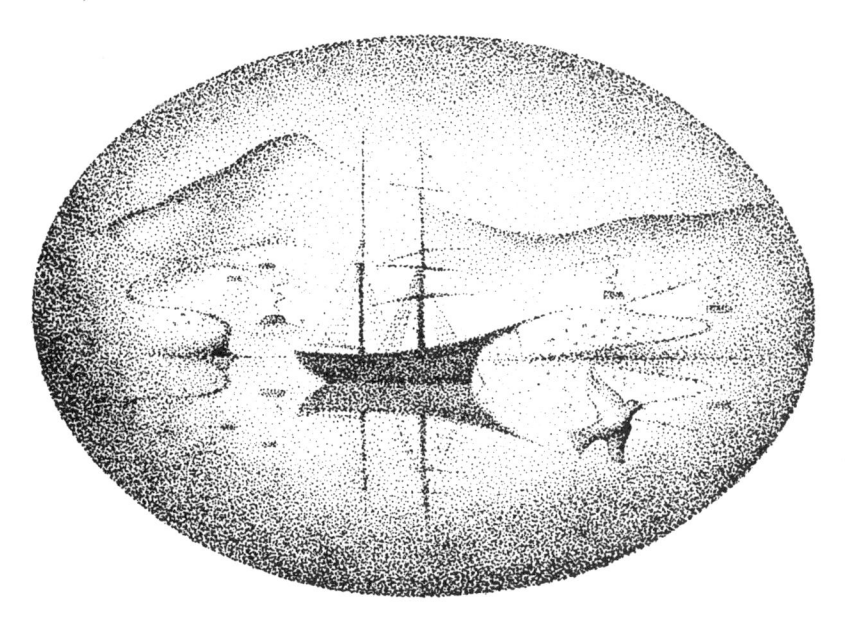

Annie took the men ashore and led them up to a grand house that she said was her home. Willie was impressed, saying: "By my faith, lass, it's no wonder that you went away, for you must be well off here." Annie replied: "Oh boy, it's refreshing to hear an oath once more, for I have never heard an oath or any swearing since I left human kind. No, no, Fin Folk do not waste their breath on swearing. So, boys, I'll tell you all, you'd better not swear while in Hilda-Land. And remember while you are here, a close tongue keeps a safe head."

They all went inside the great hall and were given plenty to eat and drink. When they had had their fill she showed them all to beds where they slept for a long time. When they awoke they found that a great feast had been prepared for them. All Annie's neighbours had been asked, and they came riding on sea horses. Annie's husband sat at the high seat and welcomed the men to Hilda-Land. When the feast was over Annie told the men that they should all go back onto their ship, for it was time for them to leave. The skipper complained that he did not know where they were, or what course to steer. "Take no thought for that," said Annie's husband, "we'll give you a pilot; his boat lies alongside your ship, and each of you must throw a silver shilling into this boat as pilot's fee."

The men all walked towards the shore, Annie and Willie walking behind, talking about old times. She sent messages to her family, but refused to go back with the ship. She said: "No, no, I'm too well off where I am to ever think of leaving it. And tell my mother that I have three bonnie bairns." She then took something out of her pouch and gave it to Willie. It was a token tied to a string of otter's hair. As she gave it to him she said: "I know you're courting Mary Foubister, and she's not sure about taking you, for she has many offers. But when you come home, put this token around her neck, and I'll warrant she'll like you better than any other man."

The men all said goodbye to Annie on the shore, and her husband rowed them out to their ship. Each crewman threw a silver shilling into the pilot's boat, and he laughed as the silver fell. There is nothing more dear to the hearts of the Fin Folk than silver money. When they were on board they were going to say farewell to the Fin man, but he said to them: "Oh, my good friends, I have long wanted to see men play at cards. Will you play one game with me before you sail?" The skipper smiled, saying: "That we will with right good will. I have a pack in the locker below." So they all went below and had a game of cards.

Now whether their drinks were drugged, or it was the magic of the Fin Folk, who can say, but they all fell into a deep sleep before the third trick was turned. Some slept with their heads on the table, some lay over their lockers, and there they all slept soundly. How long they slept they had no idea, but the skipper was the first to wake up. He went up the ladder onto deck, and what was the first thing he saw but the craigs of Gaitnip. He went below and roused the others, and when they came up on deck they found to their joy that the ship was safe and sound at anchor in Scapa Bay. The sun was glinting on the weathercock of St Magnus Cathedral, and that was a grand sight for the men to see.

They found that the Fin man had taken away the cards with him. They did not know why, but it is said that cards are the Devil's books and he may have been able to read some devilry out of them. The crew had many stories to tell about their visit to Hilda-Land. Willie Norn put the token around Mary Foubister's neck and they were married six weeks later. Annie Norn was never seen again, and if she is not dead, then she is living yet.

The Changling Twin

There was once a man and his wife who lived at Yesnaby. The wife had twins, and one of them became very ill so that they thought it would die. An old woman who was well known for her wisdom called to see them, and their ill baby. She stared at the child for a while, then she declared that this was not their boy but a changeling put in its place by the trows. She had the gift of second sight, so the man knew that what she said was true. She told him that there was something he could do to find out if it was a changeling, but he had to follow her directions closely. At a certain hour of the night the changeling would seem to be in distress, but he must not give it what it asked for. He was also to keep something burning in the fire all night, failing to do any of this would break the spell. The man did everything he was told.

That night, at the time given, there were the most terrible squeals from the bairn's bed. The bairn asked to be given a drink of water, but the father ignored it. This went on for some time and in the end the man's courage failed him and he gave the bairn a drink. This broke the spell, and the sick child went back to sleep. The next day the man went to see the old woman. She asked if the bairn had asked for anything during the night. The man told her that the bairn had asked for a drink of water and he could not refuse him. The old woman told him that this had broken the spell. She told him to go home and to follow the directions that she had given him, and the man promised to do so.

The second night, at the same time, the bairn started to shriek as if it was in agony. Again it asked to be given a drink of water, but the father paid no heed. This went on for some time before the man gave in and gave the child a drink. Once more he went to see the old woman and was told to follow the same instructions on the third night, and so he did.

The changeling started to scream and ask for a drink of water, but the man refused. His belief in the old woman's powers were strong, and this time he did not give in. After a while the bairn rose out of bed, rolled onto the floor, and with a piercing cry it disappeared up the chimney in a blue flame, and was never seen again.

The Holms of Ire

Lying off the north coast of Burness in Sanday are two small islands called the Holms of Ire. When the tide is low you can walk out to them without setting your feet wet. They were used by the local crofters to graze their sheep on, and this is a tale about one of those crofters.

A crofter from Burness had the right to graze his sheep on one of the Holms of Ire. He drove his sheep there one day, and left them to it. He had seven fine sheep, all with lambs running around their feet. On his way back he spotted a young seal lying on the shore. He quickly clubbed the animal and took it home with him. He was pleased with his luck, thinking that the selkie would make good eating as well as giving oil to burn in his cruisie lamp.

That night all the crofter's sheep disappeared from the Holm. In the morning there was no sign of them, yet the other crofters' sheep were running around unharmed. It was said that the selkie folk had taken their revenge on him for the killing of one of their own kind.

Mansie o' Fea

Where the present farm of Kierfiold in Sandwick now stands, there used to be a house belonging to a small farmer called Mansie o' Fea. He was a strange man, and there were many tales told about him. He had two wives at the same time, one human and one fairy. He was said to have three daughters by his fairy wife. One night he tried to introduce his mortal wife to her fairy rival, but with no success. His wife was fast asleep in her bed when the fairy entered the house, and no matter how hard he tried, Mansie could not wake her up until the fairy had gone. On certain nights of the year, like Halloween and Christmas, Mansie would leave out food for his fairy wife. It was always gone by the morning.

Both of Mansie's wives died, and he married a second human wife, but she was a great waster. She soon spent his money, and she was not very good with the housekeeping. She would buy a sheep's carcase for 23/6d, and roast it in big slices, holding it over the fire with the tongs. She also took to the drink, and the cost of it was ruinous to poor Mansie. Good home brewed ale was not good enough for her, oh no! She took to drinking tea! She bought it at 6/- per pound, and sugar at 1/- per pound. Poor Mansie was reduced to taking up the caisie and staff in his old age, and going begging from door to door.

Mansie was always the one who was looked for if cattle were taken ill. for he was known to be in league with the fairies and knew their tricks. He also knew how to break the spells of witches, and so he was very much in demand. People from all over the Mainland and the Isles used to come to Mansie for help, which he gave without charge. A horse that would not thrive was discovered to have been regularly ridden and galloped by the fairies. The owner was told to bar the stable door with a bible tied to the bar.

In Mansie's day some householders sold ale to the public in what was known as a "change house". There was one of these at Voy in Sandwick, and Mansie was a regular customer. One day a messenger was sent for Mansie, but he would not budge until he had had another pint. The landlady refused to give him another drop saying that he had had enough already. Mansie told her to go through into the ben end of the house and count the money in her pocket. When she returned he would be able to tell her exactly how much she had. This she did, and on her return he told her exactly how much money she had, right down to the last copper farthing. The landlady fixed him with a stony stare, saying: "The Devil take you Mansie! There's your pint and away home with you.

One day Mansie went to a local "change house" in the north end of Sandwick. He never returned, and his wife grew worried about his safety. She sent their young servant boy on horseback to the ale house to see if Mansie was alright. When he got there he discovered his master hale and hearty. The old man mounted the horse and the boy climbed up behind him, and they set off in good spirits.

They were riding home down the south side of the brae of Housegarth when Mansie asked the boy if would be afraid of seeing the fairies. The boy said that he would not, so Mansie asked if he might put his foot on one of the boy's feet. The boy agreed. and so Mansie set one of his feet on one of the boy's . All of a sudden the boy saw that the valley was full of mounted horsemen, and they were driving a cow before them. The horsemen were all heading towards the Bay of Skaill, with the cow running in front. Mansie told the boy that the cow belonged to a farmer called George Marwick who owned the farm of Bain on the north side of Sandwick. They had taken one of his cows, leaving a dead one of their own in its place. In the morning he would find one of his cows dead. And this proved to be the case, for the next morning George Marwick found one of his cows dead in the byre.

Kate Crackernuts

There was once a king and queen who ruled a country. The king had a daughter, and the queen also had one called Kate. The queen was very jealous of the king's daughter, as she was more beautiful than her own. She went to the henwife to ask her advice, and was told to send the king's daughter to her the following morning, but to make sure that she was fasting. The queen told the king's daughter to fetch eggs in the morning, and off she went. Before she left the house she managed to get herself something to eat. When she reached the henwife's house she asked her for eggs. The henwife said: "lift the lid off that pot there", which she did. Nothing happened, so the henwife told her: "Go home to your minnie, and tell her to keep the press door fastened."

When she returned home and told her stepmother what the henwife had said, she knew that she must have had something to eat. The next morning the queen watched the girl to make sure that she was fasting. She sent her back to the henwife for more eggs. On the way she met some people picking peas by the side of the road. She stopped to speak to them, and they gave her a handful of peas to eat. She went on her way, eating the peas as she walked. The henwife told her to lift the lid off the pot again, but again nothing happened.

On the third morning the queen went with her to make sure she had nothing to eat. When she lifted the lid off the pot this time off jumped her own bonnie head, and on jumped a sheep's head. Pleased with the result, the queen returned home.

The queen's daughter took a fine linen cloth and wrapped it around her sister's head. Then, hand in hand, they set off to find their fortune. They went further and further away, until they came to a king's castle. Kate knocked at the door and asked for a night's lodging for herself and a sick sister. This was agreed, on the condition that Kate would sit all night with the king's sick son. If all was well in the morning Kate would be given a bag of silver. Kate sat with the prince, and all was quiet until midnight. When twelve o'clock rang the sick prince got out of bed, dressed himself, and slipped out of the room, followed by Kate. The prince went to the stable, saddled his horse, called his hound, and jumped up onto the saddle. Kate leapt up behind him, unseen. Away they rode, through the greenwood. Kate picked nuts from the trees, filling her apron with them as they sped past. On they rode until they reached a green hill. The prince drew the bridle and spoke. "Open, open, green hill, and let the young prince in with his horse and his hound." Kate added, "and his lady behind him."

As soon as the prince had spoken, the hill opened and they passed in. A magnificent hall lay inside, all brightly lit. Many beautiful ladies surrounded the prince, and led him off to dance. Kate sat herself down unnoticed by the door, and watched. Here she saw a bairn playing with a wand, and overheard a fairy say: "Three strokes of that wand would make Kate's sick sister as bonnie as ever she was." So Kate rolled nuts to the bairn until it let the wand fall. She picked it up and put it in her apron. Then the cock crowed, and the prince hurried to his horse. Kate jumped up behind him and the two of them rode home. The prince returned to his bed and Kate sat down by the fire, cracking her nuts and eating them.

When the morning came Kate told the king that his son had had a good night, and was given a bag of silver. She agreed to sit with him for another night, but this time she was to get a bag of gold. The second night past as the first had done, and Kate was given the gold. She agreed to spend a third night with him, but this time she would only do it if she could marry the prince. All happened the same as the other two nights, but this time the bairn was playing with a bird. Kate overheard one of the fairies say,: "Three bites of that bird would make the sick prince as well as ever he was." So Kate rolled nuts to the bairn until it let the bird fall, and Kate picked it up and put it in her apron.

At cock crow they set off again, but instead of cracking her nuts by the fire Kate plucked the feathers off and cooked the bird. Soon a lovely smell filled the room. "Oh!", said the sick prince, "I wish I had a bite of that bird." So Kate gave him a bite of the bird, and he rose on one elbow. After a short time he said again: "Oh!, if I had another bite of that bird!" So Kate gave him another bite, and he sat up in bed. Then he spoke again saying: "Oh! if I had a third bite of that bird!" So Kate gave him a third bite of the bird, and the prince rose quite well. He dressed himself and sat down beside Kate by the fire. When the people came into his room in the morning they found Kate and the young prince cracking nuts together. So the sick son married the well sister, and the sick sister married the well son, and they lived happily and died happy, and never drank out of a dry cup.

The Changeling

One day two women were travelling in the Mainland. They stopped at a cottage by the road and asked if they could come in for a short rest. The woman in the cottage greeted them in friendly terms and asked them in. She went to put on the kettle to make some tea for her weary visitors. While the two women sat at the table drinking their tea they heard the strangest and most unearthly grunts coming from the box bed that was in the room. Their surprise gave way to horror when a repulsive looking creature put his head out of the bed and stared at them with great blinking eyes. "Oh, don't be frightened" said the woman, "he'll do you no harm." She ordered the monster to be quiet or she would use the whip. He returned to the back of the bed and remained still. While the women finished their drinks the woman told them her sad tale.

One harvest morning she had left the cottage to pick some cabbage from the yard. She was going to make some broth for the harvesters who were hard at work in the field. Before she left the house she had put her baby, a fine chubby boy, in the cradle. When she returned she was horrified to discover that her child was gone and a hideous creature was left in his place. She could see at once that this was not her son but a changeling. The trows had been to her home while she was out and had taken her own child away to their home.

The House of the Dead

The district of Quholm in Stromness had many ghost stories attached to it at one time. It was told that a boy was sent out to look for a horse that had gone astray. He had been walking for quite some time when a mist came down, and he lost his way. He wandered on for a while until he saw a house with the door standing wide open. He went inside and found a room full of people, among them he recognised his grandmother who had been dead for a long time.

He heard someone say: "Blow in his eyes". "What for?", asked his grandmother, "To make him blind" came the reply. His grandmother said: "Let the boy alone." and beckoned to him to come outside. Soon after that he found his way safely home. When he returned the people were relieved to see him alive and well. He thought that he had only been away for an hour or two, but he was told that he had been missing for months, and given up for dead.

The Death of the Fin King

The Fin Folk were known to be great fishermen, and to have a strange power over the fish in the sea. The people of Sandwick found this out to their cost when they had strayed onto the Fin Folk's fishing ground. The Fin King was very angry at the trespass, and he cast a spell over the fish so that not one of them would take a hook baited by a human fisherman. This caused great hardship for the people of the district as they were heavily reliant on fish for their daily food. Try as they like the fish would not take a baited line. They would swim around it, look at it, but never thought to taste it. The fish abounded, but not one could be caught.

At last the people were desperate and they went to see an old spae-wife[1] who lived at a house called Bokan in Wasbister. They told her their tale of woe, and said if they didn't get fish soon they may well starve that winter. The spae wife thought for some time and then came up with a plan. They were to take a boat that could pull six oars and crew it with seven young unmarried men, six on the oars and one steering. They must take with them four small, strongly made kegs. and row to the nearest fishing ground. The seventh man must bait the hooks as they travelled and get the gear ready. When they were at the fishing ground he was to say to the darrow stane[2], "Sae be atween me and thee." and then throw it overboard. They then had to pull the line up to clear it of the long tangles[3] that grow on the sea bed. As soon as this was done they would catch a fish. They must haul in the fish and head back for the shore to the place where the boat was launched. The Fin King would

---

[1] *A witch.*
[2] *A line sinker.*
[3] *Seaweed.*

follow them, and they had to throw a keg at him as they rowed back. This charm would break his spell over the fish around the coast.

Now they had to find a crew who were brave enough to risk the voyage. They also needed a boat. There was only one boat in the Bay of Skaill that had six oars, and it belonged to a man called Thomas Marwick who worked the farm of South Unigar. The boat was called "The Ram" and was kept in a noust at the north side of the bay. The boat and crew were eventually obtained and the gear was prepared in readiness.

The day that was planned for the venture dawned bright and clear. A large crowd of people gathered on the shore to watch the seven brave men take on the might of the Fin King. The boat was launched and the six strong men pulled at the oars until "Skerrow-Brae" came to the face of "Row". The line was baited and the words "Sae be atween me and thee" was muttered over the darrow stane. The stone was dropped into the sea, taking the line with it to the bottom. The line was pulled clear of the tangles and the fish was caught, just as the spae wife had predicted.

No sooner had they pulled the fish over the side than they saw the Fin King, foaming with rage. The six men pulled at the oars for all that they were worth, while the lad in the stern threw a keg to "Old Finnie". The Fin King seized the keg and crushed it to pieces in a pig's whisper. The oarsmen pulled with all their might while this was going on. "Old Finnie" made short work of the first keg and was soon after them again, as swift as an otter. The steersman threw a second keg at him, and again he tore it to bits with rage. The people on the shore were leaping up and down with excitement. The men shouted, the women shrieked and the babies screamed. The minister stood on the kirk brae, shouting: "Head for the holy house" and wildly pointing at the kirk. The steersman followed his instructions, and pointed the boat in that direction. Meanwhile his majesty had finished tearing at the second keg and was on his way again. As he came up to the boat the lad threw the third keg into the sea. This time he didn't stop to crush it but carried on going, crunching it as he swam. The people on the shore were horrified to see the Fin King catching up with the boat. One of the people who was there that day said that he was as big as a peat stack.

Things were looking bad for the boat and its crew as they were still some distance from the shore, and "Old Finnie" was close on their heels. The Fin King lunged at the stern of the boat, his jaws were open and his webbed hand was about to seize hold of the brave little vessel. The man who was pulling the stroke oar was called Johnnie Brass. He took hold of the last keg and threw it with all his might at the monster's head, smashing his skull. The boat grounded on the sandy shore and many willing hands pulled it up the beach to safety.

Young Johnnie Brass was hailed as a hero by all the people there. The minister said that there would always be people of the name of Brass at the north side of the Bay of Skaill as long as grass grew or water ran. Now young Johnnie had a sweetheart by the name of Jeanie Irvine, and her mother pushed her way through the crowd and flung her arms around his neck. She said that even if her Jeanie was twice as good and bonnie he would be worthy of her.

The carcase of the Fin King was pulled from the sea and laid on a large pile of stones at the north side of the bay. Wood, heather, peats and dried tangles were gathered and heaped over his body and set alight until he was reduced to ashes. A cairn was raised over the spot where "Old Finnie" was burnt, as a memorial to that day. So that people should not forget the event, the burn of Rin, where the people who were cremating the Fin King drank, was renamed Snoosgarth, and the stones from the pyre was called the Castle of Snoosgarth. The name came from the snoosing or snorting noises that the dying creature made. You can still see the stones there that were burnt in the fire.

From that day onwards there were plenty of fish in the sea for the people to catch. It was said that the luckiest boat of all was "The Ram", and Thomas Marwick did well from the adventure. The old spae-wife had always said that "a ram would doose[4] the Fin King over."

Johnnie Brass married Jeanie Irvine the following winter. They were wed at the kirk at Skaill while a gale raged from the west outside. This did not stop the wedding party from gaily stepping out, with a fiddler from Harray leading the way. They marched to the top of Sandfiold Hill where the fiddler played "Weel may the boaty row". The people danced so hard that between them and the gale there was hardly a grain of sand left on the top of the hill. The wind blew the sand into the valley and completely buried a house called the Fan. They then went to the bride's home in Newgarth, called Saenia. The minister declared that the house should be renamed Host Snoca in honour of Johnnie's brave deed.

Host referred to the dying coughs and Snoca the last snorting of the Fin King. The minister insisted that he should have the first dance with the bride, as it was thought to bring luck to the happy couple. The dancing and drinking lasted all night. When the minister finally left he said "Sae be atween ye baith." meaning may you always enjoy plenty, and that they did.

---

[4] *Butt.*

The Fairies Fishing Trip

There was once a man who lived at Windwick on the east side of South Ronaldsay. Like many of the people who lived in the area he had a boat in which he went fishing. The boat was housed in a noust by the bay, and he used to go and look at her every day. He made sure that everything was in order and that there was no water lying in her.

One day the man was very surprised to find that his boat was wet, like she had been to sea. The other boats in the other nousts were bone dry, only his boat was wet. He could not understand this, but he was determined to find out the reason. He decided that he would keep watch all night, hidden in the boat.

That night he went and hid inside his boat, and waited. He did not have long to wait before he heard voices approaching. Soon the voices were all around the boat, and he felt the boat moving down the beach towards the sea. The man remained out of sight. for he now knew that it was the fairies that had been using his boat. The boat was soon in the sea and the fairies were pulling at the oars on their way to the fishing grounds.

After a while the fairies stopped rowing, and the boat drifted with the swell. They tasted the water, but said: "We'll have to go further." So they set off again, pulling at the oars for what seemed like ages. Once more they stopped and tasted the water. "Na, no fish here," they declared, and off they went for a third time. A while later they stopped again, tasted the water and said: "Ah, yes! There's fish here." and the fairies started their night's fishing. The man stayed covered, but he heard one of the fairies say:

"The Braes O' Mar on Swithomaswee,
There'll be fish there to our dying day!"

The Broonie of Copinsay

Off the south east coast of the Mainland lies the beautiful little green island of Copinsay. The high sea-cliffs at its southern end are home to thousands of pairs of breeding sea birds. There is one house on the island, and a lighthouse that lights the way for those who toil on the sea. It is now uninhabited, though it used to be home to quite a few people.

A very long time ago there was a farmer who lived alone on the island of Copinsay. His only company were the sea birds who nested on its steep cliffs, and the few animals that he tended.

One winter's night the farmer was tired from his hard day's work, and had gone to bed around 10 o'clock. It was a box-bed, which was enclosed and helped to keep out the draughts. As he lay in his bed he thought of his sweetheart that he would soon wed and bring to the island. He dozed off to sleep, but woke later with a start as he could see a figure standing in the corner of the room near the door. He raised his head to have a better look and was greeted with a sight that would make most men's hair stand on end. It was a creature like a man, only smaller, very clumsy looking and as naked as the day it was born. Its wet skin was like leather and it had a slightly phosphorescent glow. Its bald head was as flat as a pan-cake, and instead of hair it had seaweed.

The farmer was shocked by the sight of the creature, but he was a man with a fiery temper and was quick to take action. Remembering that steel and the word of God was a good protection from evil, he seized a razor from the shelf beside his bed, took a psalm book from under his pillow, and jumped to the floor to do battle. He crossed himself with the psalm book. and cut a circle in the air with the razor. The intruder made no attempt to attack, but stood gibbering at him from the corner of the room. The farmer picked up the fire tongs and poker from beside the fire and threw it with all his might at the creature's head, but it was too fast for him and they missed. The man then grasped the heavy crook[1] from above the fire and lunged at his foe.

The crook was not made of steel but soft iron from the smithy. The creature plucked it from the man's hand and tossed it aside. The farmer fell on his opponent with his bare fists, punching it twice before it darted out of the door.

---

[1] *A chain suspended above the fire on which pots were hung.*

The man went and sat down on his straw-backed stool by the fire to gather his wits. As he sat he thought about the creature, and as his temper cooled it dawned on him that it had not once tried to do him any harm. After some time the creature poked its head through the door and smiled. It slowly entered the room, still smiling and making friendly gestures to the man. He sat quite still in his chair and tried to understand what it was that the creature was saying.

The broonie, as he was later called, said that his name was Hughbo and that he lived in the sea. He said he was sick of living there and gnawing on dead men's bones and he wanted to live on land. He asked the farmer if he might let him stay on Copinsay, and he was willing to work for his keep. Every night he would grind enough oats in the quern for the farmer's morning porridge. All he wanted in return was a saucer of milk to sup with his own handful of burstin[2].

This proposition was accepted by the farmer, who was a kind man at heart. He was also a busy man, and the thought of his breakfast meal being ready for him in the morning was very appealing. He soon got used to the appearance of the broonie, and the bargain was struck. The farmer went back to his bed and lay there for some time listening to the low gritty chuckle of the quern. In the morning there was a bowl of freshly ground meal waiting for him. Hughbo became a valued and faithful servant around the farm. In the long winter nights the farmer would talk to him by the fireside, or as often as not he would lie in bed and watch the clumsy phosphorescent figure at work with the quern.

Now the farmer's thoughts turned to his sweetheart who lived on the Mainland. It occurred to him that he had better tell her about his unusual servant before they were wed. She was fearful at first about meeting the broonie, but the farmer talked about Hughbo in glowing terms. He said he was faithful, hard working and honest. She went with him to visit Copinsay, and Hughbo. She did not like the look of him at first, but his good natured way helped her to overcome her fears. She made several trips to Copinsay, and said she had no objection to either the island or Hughbo. The wedding day was set, and the farmer soon had a bride to take home with him.

[2] *Barley dried in a pot.*

They spent their days in wedded bliss, love went hand in hand with the daily toil of the farm. They never had very much time to spare for Hughbo, they only had eyes for each other. But Hughbo did not mind for he was happy with his task of grinding the meal for both their breakfasts. However the young woman could not get used with Hughbo's nakedness, and his ugly form and flat head repulsed her. She would lie in bed at night watching him at work turning the quern. His nakedness started to bother her, so she decided that he would have to cover himself up.

Without telling her husband she got an old cloak with a hood to cover the broonie's bald head. One night, after the farmer had gone to bed, she placed the garment on the quern, went to bed and waited for the broonie to find her gift. Hughbo usually come in quietly to grind the meal, but this night he was no sooner in the door than he let out a great wail. He ran round and round the quern, sobbing his heart out and saying over and over again:

"Hughbo's gotten a cloak and hood,
So Hughbo can do no more good."

He then ran out of the door and into the dark night and was never seen on Copinsay again.

The Good Neighbours of Greenie Hill

There was once a blind man who lived at Norton in Birsay, and they called him Blind Tom. One evening Tom left his home to walk over to the houses of Greenie that lay about half a mile away. He was looking forward to spending a few hours happily chatting with his friends. He had hardly left his door when he heard a sound like a lot of pigs running around his feet. He gave them a wallop with his stick. he thought that there must be hundreds of them. He grabbed one of them by the tail and jumped onto its back. They all headed for the knowes of Furs-a-Kelda where Tom heard the finest fiddling that he had ever heard in his life.

He got down off the pig and started to dance. There were lots of people there, but when Tom tried to take hold of one they slipped through his fingers like water. He danced and better danced, heuched and danced, and so did everyone else. He refused to take a drink from them, but went down to the well of Furs-a-Kelda when he was thirsty.

When Tom rejoined the dancing one of the dancers came up to him and said. "Now, Tom, do not take any of their meat or drink, or if you do you will never get back to Norton. Put this in your pocket, and see what it will be when you get home. Slip it in your pocket and put up your hand to your mouth the same as if you were eating, they are watching us." Tom did as he was told, for he knew who it was who talked to him. He was the son of a family from across the loch who had been changed[1] by the fairies when he was just a baby.

The next morning Tom's father took a look through his pockets. He found them to be full of sheep and horse dung, and when he held it in his hands it melted away into smoke leaving a strong smell of sulphur in the house. And that was the story of Tom's night out with the good neighbours.

[1] *Stolen and replaced by a fairy "changeling".*

The Fairy Battle

One morning a farmer at Greenie Hill was having his breakfast when the dog started to bark. The barking was both loud and fierce, so the farmer went out to see what was troubling the dog. He called to him, but the dog paid no attention. He was snapping at something and he looked as if he was trying to stop someone from entering the gate.

The farmer could see nothing, but he could hear something very strange. The sound of men marching filled the air, like the sound of the Orkney Volunteers on the move. The man felt himself stuck to the ground, while the dog still kept on barking. All of a sudden he saw a troop of men marching past. It was six deep and about seventy yards in length, and the men were carrying guns over their shoulders. The officers carried drawn swords in their hands. They marched along the road, about sixty yards from where the farmer stood. When they came to the dyke at the public road the officer in front laid his sword on the dyke, like he was directing the men to march through it. When all the men came to the dyke they disappeared. When the last man had vanished the dog stopped barking and went into the house. When the farmer went to the spot where the men had marched through the dyke he found a few of the top stones had been knocked into the ditch beside it.

The farmer thought that he had seen a very strange sight, but his story had a twist in its tail. A friend of his told him that another man had seen something similar. This man had been standing on the rising ground above the knowes of Furs-a-Kelda. He saw a body of men coming out of a small knowe in the farm of Norton. They marched out of the mound straight towards the knowes of Furs-a-Kelda. When they were about half way there the knowes of Furs-a-Kelda opened and out marched another company of men. When the two sides met there was a terrible battle, with many men killed and wounded on both sides. After the battle was over the remaining men marched back to their knowes, while some of them carried the dead and wounded from the field. The second farmer's description of the men matched what the first farmer had seen, even the dress that they wore was the same, but at that time neither of these farmers knew what the other had seen.

The Breckness Mermaid

One fine summer's day, a Breckness man was walking along shore He was enjoying the view, as the sun sparkled on the Atlantic waves and the huge red cliffs of Hoy rose from the sea like a giant castle wall. The only sound was the cry of the seagulls that circled above his head and the gentle motion of the waves among the rocks. He lay down on the grassy shore and gazed across the wide ocean that stretched to the horizon.

As he lay there, he saw a sight more beautiful than anything that he had ever seen before. A mermaid was bathing in the sea, right before where he lay. Her face was the most beautiful face that the young man had ever seen, and her golden hair flowed over her milk white back like spun gold. Never had he seen a creature so lovely, and his heart was lost to her.

On a rock next to where the mermaid swam there lay her sea skin. The young man knew that if he could get possession of that skin, the mermaid could not return to her home under the sea. She would be in his power and would have to follow him back home to his house. He left the spot where he lay, and crept down the shore like a cat. The mermaid had now left the sea. and was combing her long golden hair. The man was so near to her now that he snatched the skin and hid it under his clothes. At that moment the mermaid saw him, and turned to seize her skin; but it was gone. The tears rolled down her lovely face as she stared at the man who was the cause of her sorrow. She pleaded with him to give her back her skin so that she could return to the friendly waves, but he refused. He wished her to come home with him and be his bride, but she refused. After some time she finally agreed, and they both went to his house.

They were married, and lived together for a number of years. They had six fine children, three boys and three girls. These children were said to be the bonniest bairns in all of Orkney. When they grew up, their mother tried to get them to discover where their father kept her stolen sea skin. After being questioned about the skin for some time, the man finally told his favourite daughter where he hid it. She ran to her mother, delighted at her success in finding out this information. Soon after hearing the news, the mermaid disappeared. Many long hours the man spent wandering the shore where he had first seen his mermaid wife, but she was never there. The birds still circled over his head as they had done long ago. but the mermaid did not come back to comb her golden hair in the warm sunshine.

One day the man was hiding behind some large rocks on the shore when he saw the mermaid come out of the sea. Her children ran down the shore towards her, and she sat and combed their hair. As soon as the man appeared, she returned to the sea. Many times she returned to that spot to comb the children's hair, but she made sure that her sea skin was close by her hand. Tradition has it that if you go down to the shore at Breckness you can still hear the sweet song of the mermaid. It was said to be an old Norse sea-song that she used to lull her little ones to sleep. The echoes of the song can never die, but will forever drift around the rocks and caverns of the deep.

Davie o' Teeveth

About two hundred years ago there lived a man in the parish of Harray called Davie o' Teeveth. Davie was a weaver and taylor by trade, but he and his wife Jenny also ran an ale house at Teeveth. Gin was smuggled in from Evie, and Davie was very partial to a drop. Jenny though, had other plans. She kept the gin locked up for the customers. Davie complained that bread and milk would not satisfy him, even ale made him thirsty, he wanted gin. This led to strife between him and his wife. One day he told Jenny that we was going to commit suicide by drowning himself. He ran down to the burn at the Pow o' Pulpeuggs and jumped in. When someone went to look for him later they found him sitting quite cosy on a dry ledge under the banks of the burn.

Davie had a reputation of having second sight, and being in league with the fairies. Now it happened that one of Davie's four daughters was being courted by a young man called Baronet Mackerry Macwhurry. He claimed to be the son of a wealthy gentleman, and Jenny was very impressed. Davie on the other hand knew that the young man was not what he seemed, and took a dislike to him. He said that he had had dreams about him, and they were bad omens. Nobody paid any heed to Davie, and the wedding was arranged. On the booking night Jenny went through to the ben end of the house to tell Davie that the young man had arrived, and for him to come through and see him. Davie replied: "I would rather you would try to pick the eyes out of my head." Shortly after, Mr Macwhurry disappeared, along with a considerable sum of money that Davie's daughter had saved. The young woman went to Edinburgh, and found a good job in service.

Near the croft of Teeveth stood a mound called Dunshou, which was the home of the local fairies. Davie was much in demand as a fiddle player, and was a great favourite at rants and weddings. On winter nights he would go to Dunshou with his fiddle. He said that the fairies would let him in through one side of the mound, and let him out the through the other side. After a wedding he would take his fiddle to Dunshou to play a few tunes before going home. "I always have to go and give the peedie folk a dance." he would say.

A Harray man was going home from a wedding one night, and his road took him past the Knowe of Hammeran near the lands of Overhouse. As he got nearer he thought he could hear music, so he went for a closer look. At first he thought that it was still the sound of the fiddle music he had heard at the wedding ringing in his ears. As he got closer he saw that it was Davie o' Teeveth sitting playing his fiddle. Davie greeted him, saying: "Sit you down? Jamie, beside me." Jamie did as he was told. After a while Davie broke the silence. "There they come now; there they gather, do you not see them." Jamie found the bonnet on his head starting to rise, and he took to his heels and ran.

Later on in life Davie took a great dislike to his fiddle, and he swore that he would never lay a finger on it again. When asked why, he would reply: "The Devil's in her." A young Harray man called to ask Davie if he would sell his fiddle, and Davie agreed. He picked the fiddle up between the toes of the fire tongs, and presented it to the young man.

Davie and Jenny spent their final days in the town of Stromness. Davie was said to be in touch with people who were long since dead. He made the prophesy that there would be an eight roomed house on Dunshou, and sure enough the United Free Church Manse was built on the site. It is now a private house, called Holland House. He also predicted that one day apples would grow on the brae of Dunshou and the gates of Nettletar. They were two very unlikely spots for apple cultivation in Davie's day, but his prophesies came true.

Building the Cathedral

St Magnus Cathedral was founded by the Norse Jarl Rognvald Kolsson in 1137. It is dedicated to his saintly uncle, who was murdered in Egilsay in c1116. There is a rather unusual tale regarding how the red sandstone that it is built from was obtained.

Women walked to Hoy for the red sandstone that was used to build St Magnus Cathedral in Kirkwall. They walked over the sea in Scapa Flow to reach the island, and carried the stones back in their brattos (a coarse apron). Back and fore they went, over the sea. One day they were told that the building was finished, and they did not need any more stones. They were half way across the Flow at the time, and they all tipped the stones out at the one place. This was how the skerry called The Barrel of Butter was made.

The Stolen Winding Sheet

There was once a woman who lived at Bea in Sanday. Her father had been called Black Jock, and the name had been passed on to his daughter, though her real name was Jenny. Black Jock was a hard, rough character who supplemented her living by being a howdy-wife. She took people into the world and made sure they were decently put out of it too.

Baubie Skithawa was a frail, feeble old woman, and had been for so many years. Knowing that the end was near, she made all the arrangements for her funeral. She had bought a length of fine material from a man who had a stall at the Lammas Market in Kirkwall. With this cloth she had made herself a winding sheet to wear in her grave.

Some time before she died, Baubie called for Black Jock to pay a visit. She was a proud woman and did not want to be beholden to anyone. "Lass I'm wanting to show you where all my grave boonies[1] are lying, so you may know where to lay your hands on them when they're needed. And I would like to know if I have all that I need, and if you think the clothes will do alright. For you know, I always liked to be decent, and I would not like to go to the grave in poor boonie. Do you think I would need to try them on?" "No, no" said Black Jock, "I know fine by the look of my own eyes whether they'll do or not." Black Jock thought that she had never seen such a bonnie winding sheet in her life before. She had laid out many bodies in her time, but Baubie would be the finest dressed of them all.

At last, word came that old Baubie Skithawa had died. Black Jock laid out the corps and dressed it in the lovely winding sheet. She was present at the "kistin"[2], and took her turn for two nights sitting with the body. This was called the "leek wak" and was very important, for

[1] *Good clothes, shroud.*
[2] *When the body is placed in the coffin.*

evil spirits may steal away the body before it's safe in consecrated soil.

On the day of the funeral Black Jock drank like a beast. She was seen to be always fingering the winding sheet, and muttering to herself. She said to Baubie Croy, "Sal[3], it's a great pity to put such a good piece of cloth in the ground." Now Black Jock had the reputation of being in league with the Devil, and she must have been to have done what she did. That night, when all the good people of Sanday were asleep in bed, Black Jock sneaked out of her house. She took a spade and walked to the kirkyard of the parish of Cross. When she arrived there she set to work with the spade and dug up poor old Baubie Skithawa's grave. When the coffin was uncovered, she broke open the lid and stole the winding sheet from off the body. She filled up the grave again and returned home with her prize which she placed in the bottom of a large kist.

The next day Lady Hellsness[4] sent her servant Andrew Moodie on an errand to Lady Clestran of Stove. She had wanted some barm[5] to make ale with. This was a long journey on foot, and it was getting dark by the time Andrew headed for home. The sky was growing blacker by the minute, and as Andrew reached the Sand o' Bea there broke out a terrible thunder storm. The thunder roared and the lightning danced and flashed. Sometimes the lightning struck the ground, sometimes out at sea, sometimes it leapt from one cloud to another. It was the worst storm that Andrew had ever seen in all his born days.

As he battled his way through the storm, Andrew noticed that the sky was blackest over the Cross kirk. The road that he was walking passed right by its gate. As he approached the kirk he saw a sight that nearly put him out of his mind. There was a pillar of fire soaring up from every grave that lay around the kirk. They looked like ships masts, but glowed red, yellow and blue. They were so tall that they were higher than the roof of the kirk. Sometimes they stood up straight, and sometimes they swayed to and fro. On top of these pillars of fire stood the spirits of the dead. One, two, or even three or four ghosts on every pillar. They

[3] *Soul, used as a mild oath.*
[4] *Elsness.*
[5] *Working yeast.*

seemed to be talking to each other, as their dead clothes fluttered in the breeze. Some waved and beckoned to one another while others just shook their heads.

Among these spirits there was one that was naked. It was the ghost of Baubie Skithawa who had her winding sheet stolen. It seemed that the other spirits were making fun of her, for it is said that if the dead return to earth they take with them their old ways. Andrew thought that Baubie's ghost was turning its head to look at him. He knew that the stare of a ghost was something best avoided, for it can turn a man mad. Instead of waiting for a message he turned on his heels and ran for all that he was worth, straight to the house of Bea.

When Andrew reached the door he found it barred. He hammered on the door with both his fists and feet, and shouted: "For the Lord of heaven's sake, open the door. I have seen a sight tonight that I will never be the better of all my life. If you ever think to get mercy yourself, have mercy upon me, and open the door. No! I never saw the like in all my life. But I need not speak of life, for death's on my back."

Black Jock was in the house by herself as her husband was visiting a sick cousin at Rusness. The goodman of Bea was a poor witless creature. Black Jock had driven the last little bit of sense that he had out of him, and that was not much anyway. So instead of leaving some gifts of food or drink for the invalid, he had invited himself to stay. After what seemed like a lifetime to Andrew, Black Jock unbarred the door and let him in. She replaced the bar, and Andrew noticed that it had three awls sticking out of it. "What Devil's taken you out on such a night? Idle whalp that you are! Sit there on the stool, and remember, a close tongue keeps a safe head." The moment she said the Devil's name there was such a roar of thunder right over the house that Andrew thought the roof would fall. The lightning flashed so bright all around the house that he was both stunned and blinded.

When he recovered his senses he looked around the house. The peat fire burned in the middle of the floor, but the smoke hole in the roof had been filled up as tightly as it could possibly be. So had the window hole, for glass was uncommon in those days and only the rich could afford it. There was a hole through a flagstone in the roof above the door that served as a door to the cat. It too was blocked up, and the cat lay shaking

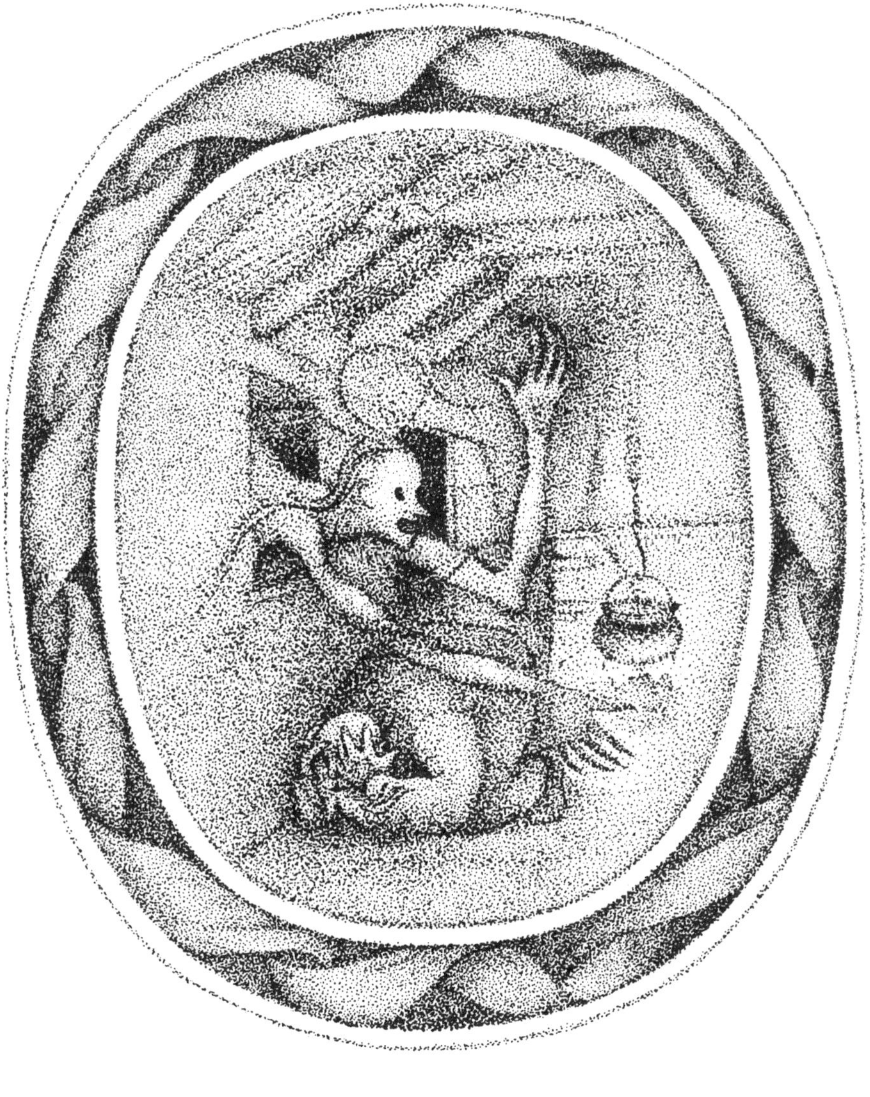

with fear in the corner. Black Jock was sitting in the middle of the floor, drawing a circle around herself with a large needle. All the time her mouth was moving, but Andrew could not hear what she was saying for the thunder was so loud. He was just about to tell her what he'd seen at the kirkyard when, as soon as he opened his mouth, she threw a peat at him. It hit his knee with such force that he let out a yell of pain.

He had little time to worry about the pain. Between every clap of thunder he heard a sound like a thousand scolding voices approaching the house. He could hear them speak, but he could not understand a word that they said for it was no earthly tongue that they spoke. The packing in the smoke hole, the window hole and the cat hole was torn out, but not by mortal hands. To his horror Andrew could see the face of Baubie Skithawa at the window, and it was as white as chalk. And as the ghost peered in at the window, it called out: "Cold, cold am I this night! It's cold, cold to lie in the earth mother naked! Give me my sheet!" All the time she gave out a piercing shriek that was not like any earthly sound.

One of the ghosts put its hand through the cat hole above the door and pulled out the sickle that was sticking there. It soon let it drop though, for there was steel in the hook and ghosts can't bear the touch of it. The ghost yelled in pain and this seemed to give them all a scare. After they got over this fright they became angry. Round and round the house they danced, and over the house, and on the house, and even under the house they went. As they went they roared like mad bulls.

Now it was nearing cock crow, and the ghosts knew that their time was running out. Baubie Skithawa stuck her white face through the window and stretched out her long neck. She managed to get her long white arms through the window hole too and she waved them about, this way and that. She stared all around the room, as though she was looking for something. Andrew was cowering on the floor in mortal fear of Baubie's ghost. He could feel the breeze from her arms as they swept through the air. It was then that he got a wallop from Baubie's ghost, right on the top of his head. He fainted as soon as it happened, and his foot caught Black Jock on the hand, knocking the needle from out of her grasp.

Wanting steel, Black Jock was in a dangerous position. If the ghosts got a hold of her they would tear her to shreds. She had no time to waste. She cleared the top of the large kist and opened it. She dug down to the bottom of it and pulled out Baubie Skithawals stolen winding sheet. As she did this the winding sheet flew from her hand like a living thing. It shot up the smoke hole in a blue flame. "The Devil go and stay with you!", said Black Jock. The words were hardly out of her mouth when something gave her a wallop on the back that knocked her to the floor.

Just at that moment the cock crowed, and the ghosts flew away back to their own place like a flock of swans. When people came to the house of Bea the next day they found it in an awful state, and there were three cows dead in the byre. Andrew was lying on the floor like a man half dead. He had the marks of Baubie's thumb and finger on his head, and the hair never grew on that spot again.

Black Jock was also lying on the floor where the spirits had left her, and was unable to stand. The people tried to lift her, but with no success. Five women and three men pulled for all that they were worth, but they could not move her for she was ghost bound. The people did not want to call the minister for they thought that he would not like the situation. In the end they called on old Mansie Peace, the grandfather of Paetie Peace who would neither drown or burn. He said seven prayers over her, then took seven blue stones and boiled them up to make "forspoken water". He poured the forspoken water over Black Jock's back, and this lifted the spell. If you don't believe my tale, just remember one thing. There's more things in heaven and hell than we understand here on earth.

The Evie Man's Dance

Three Evie men sailed to Kirkwall on business. The weather had turned bad so they were forced to return home by land. It was a long journey made all the more tiring by the fact that each man had to carry a sack on his back.

As they passed the mound of Howan Greeny they looked in and saw the fairies dancing. One of the men said that he would like to join in the dance, and ran into the mound. He danced for such a long time that his friends asked him to leave with them and return home. Every time they asked him he made the same reply: "Wait till the reel's ended." After waiting for quite some time the two men turned and went home, leaving their friend dancing in the mound.

Two years later the two men were on a journey that passed the mound of Howan Greeny. When they looked inside they saw their friend still dancing with the fairies. They called to him, and he answered: "Bless me, have you not gone home yet!" They asked him if he was not ready to go home yet, to which he replied: "Wait till the reel's ended." The two men went into the mound and pulled their friend out of the charmed circle.

Boray Isle

The little island of Gairsay rises from the sea like a hill surrounded by water. It has a few small holms dotted around its coast. The second largest is called the Holm of Boray, and it is the setting for the following tale.

It was a fine summer's evening, and Harold of Gairsay was out in his boat at the fishing. It grew late, and as the sun set in the west he heard the most wonderful music. He had never heard the like of it before and he turned his boat to follow the sound. It took him to the small island of Boray where he saw a group of people dancing. They were all very grandly dressed and clearly having a fine time. Harold looked and looked, but he could not see any musicians on the island. They were either invisible or the music was created by magic.

He took his boat close to the shore to have a better look. On the shore was a group of black objects, like beasts. He went ashore and picked one up to see what it was. It was a seal skin. He watched the dancers for a while as they whirled around and around. When the sun rose over the horizon the music suddenly stopped and the dancers all hurried to the shore. Harold dropped the seal skin into his boat, pushed it off, and rowed away from the shore. At a little distance he stopped to see what would happen next. The dancers all seized their seal skins, put them on, and jumped into the sea. They were all swimming around now in the form of seals. All that is except for one woman. She was left alone, searching along the shore for the skin that Harold had taken.

Harold turned his boat back towards to the island to talk to the woman. When he drew near her he got the fright of his life, for the woman was no other than his own dead mother. She had been drowned many years before. She told Harold that it was the fate of all drowned people to become seals. but they could return to their human form for one night every month. On that night they could dance from sunset to sunrise, but they had to return back to the sea afterwards. She begged Harold for the return of her skin, but he refused. He did not want to lose his mother for a second time. In the end he agreed, but only after she promised him the bonniest lass among all the selkie folk as his wife. He was told to return to the island in one month's time when she would show him the young woman's skin. If he took her skin she would be in his power for as long as he kept the skin safely locked away. Harold said farewell to his mother, and they parted.

On the night appointed Harold returned to the island of Boray. Again the same lovely music was playing and the mysterious dancers were back. He landed his boat unseen and his mother came down to the shore and touched a skin lying on the beach. Harold took it and set it in his boat. He returned to his home in Gairsay where he hid the skin. Before sunrise he returned to the island and waited.

Just as before the music stopped as the sun peeped over the horizon. The dancers put on their seal skins and disappeared into the sea. One beautiful young woman was left on the beach, wringing her hands and crying. Her skin had gone and she could not join her own people. After a time Harold went back for her, and they talked. She said that she was the daughter of a pagan king. He tried to comfort her and persuaded her to return to his house and become his bride.

Harold loved her dearly, and they had several children. After a while she became sick, it was as if she was wasting away with some secret grief. She often asked Harold for her seal skin, but he could not bear to lose her and so he refused. At last she confessed that she was worried about her soul, because she was a pagan. A priest was called and she was baptised as a Christian, but this still did not stop her from pining away.

"Harold," she said one day, "I've have lived long and happily together. If we part, we part forever. If I die I cannot be sure that my soul is saved, for I have long lived a pagan. Tonight is the dancing night; roll me in my seal skin and leave me on the beach. They cannot take me away if I am Christian. But you must go out of sight, and return for me in the morning; then you will know my fate."

Sadly Harold agreed to his wife's wishes. He took her to Boray and laid her on the shore wrapped in her seal skin. He went to the other side of Gairsay to wait for the sunrise. He sat all night with his head in his hands. The silence was broken by a sudden wail, they had found her on the shore. It was midsummer, when the nights are short and it never get dark, but that night seemed endless to Harold. At last the dawn broke and Harold set off to the island. He found her where he had left her on the shore, but she was dead. They had not been able to take her away with them, for she was a Christian. On her sweet face she wore a smile, the sign of a soul at peace. That smile comforted Harold, for he now knew that their parting would not be forever.

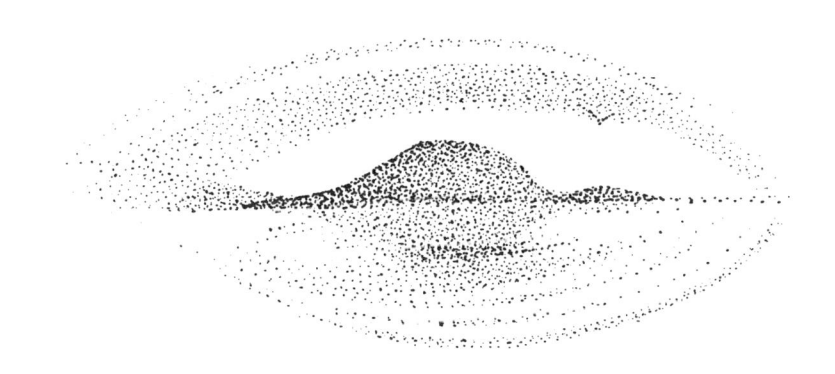

The Trows of Huip

The farm of Huip in Stronsay has many tales of trows. They used to help the farmer out around the farm. One evening, at harvest time, the farmer had a field full of sheaves to set up into stooks. He set up one stook, then said: "All like this." In the morning the whole field was stooked.

The trows were rewarded for their work with food. The farmer would throw some food over his shoulder at meal times and say: "This one's for you Kork. This one's for you Tring." and the food would disappear.

The trows did cause trouble sometimes, and the last thing that the farmer and his family would do at night was to "buil the trows". That means pen them in for the night. They did this by forming a circle around the mound that the trows lived in. They each carried a tin pail or a pot or pan, anything that could make a noise. They would then beat them with sticks, walking forward as they did so, driving the trows to their home deep within the knowe. They could then expect to get a peaceful night's sleep.

Hether Blether

A very long time ago there lived a young woman in the island of Rousay. One fine day she went to the hill to cut peats. When her work was done she sat down among the heather to rest. She was surprised to see that she was not alone, for there was a strange man on the hill too. He came towards her and started to talk. They sat there chatting away for quite some time. At last the man asked the girl if she would come home with him. She refused at first, but the man had a silver tongue and he soon gained her trust and she went with him.

When she never returned that night her family became worried. A search party was formed and they set out for the hill. They looked here, they looked there, but there was no sign of the girl anywhere. It was with heavy hearts that they returned to their homes that night. There were no hearts heavier than those of the girl's own family.

A long time after, the girl's father and brother went to sea to fish. When they had travelled a good way to the west of Eynhallow a thick fog rolled in around them. It was so thick that they could see nothing and they had no idea where they were. At last the boat touched land. They jumped over the side of the boat and pulled it up the shore. The only place it could be was Eynhallow, so they set off in search of shelter.

Out of the mist they could see the shape of a large house ahead of them. It was like no house that was on Eynhallow, they were sure of that. They went up to the house to see if anyone lived there. The old man knocked on the door and waited for a reply. Who should answer the door but his own daughter who had been lost in the hills all those years before. They greeted each other with many hugs and kisses and words of joy. She took them in and made them something to eat. She told them that she was married to a sea man who was a very good husband to her.

As they talked a great brown wisp of heather simmans[1] came rolling in and went through the house to the ben end. In a few minutes a tall handsome man came back into the room. He was introduced as the girl's husband, and greeted his in-laws with great kindness. Two more heather simmans rolled in, and out of them came two more sea men who had been out fishing.

After a pleasant visit the fog cleared a little, so the men had to say farewell. The old man pleaded with his daughter to return with them, but she said that she was happy living there with her husband. She did give her father a knife, telling him that as long as he had it he would always have luck with the fishing. He could also use it to find his way back to see her again whenever he pleased. They said a sad goodbye on the shore, then gripped the gunwales of the boat and pushed her back into the sea. As the boat pushed off the old man let slip the knife and it sank to the bottom of the sea. In a moment the boat reached the Rousay shore and the island had disappeared. The island of Hether Blether can still sometimes be seen west of Eynhallow, but remains untrod by human foot.

[1] *A home made rope, usually made from twisted straw.*

Tammy Hay and the Fairies

Tammy Hay was the miller at the old meal mill in the township of Ireland in Stenness. He lived at Breckan, and was generally called "The man o' Breckan". Tammy was always seeing fairies, though people thought that this had more to do with the time he spent drinking in the public houses than with the supernatural. He was married to Margid Clouston in 1745, and they had a daughter in 1751. A couple of days after the birth, Tammy was heading home from the mill in the evening. He had had a few drinks and was as happy as a dog with two tails. His road home was a winding path that stretched up the side of the hill. The road took him near the old mound at Tongue, which was known to be the home of a group of fairies.

As Tammy stopped at the foot of the brae he could hear voices, it was fairies talking among themselves. Tammy stood and listened for a while and what he heard made his hair rise. The fairies were on their way to Breckan to steal his newborn baby daughter. They had with them a sickly, dying brat of their own and they were going to change it for Tammy's bairn.

Tammy took to his heels and ran home as fast as he could. He got there just before the fairies arrived. so he had no time to waste. He took down the family bible and the gully[1] from above the fire. As the fairies came through the door he beat the gully on the bible and muttered a prayer. The fairies ran screaming from the house back to their mound. As they ran they argued amongst themselves as to which one of them had spoken so loudly that Tammy had found out what they were planning.

On another occasion Tammy was walking home one night when he saw a group of fairies dancing around their hillock. He felt himself being

[1] *A large knife.*

drawn towards them. When he got up to the mound he saw that the side of it was open. Inside was a whole host of fairies dancing for all that they were worth. Before he knew what had happened, Tammy found himself in the mound dancing with the fairies. He danced the night away and left at first light. Although he had been dancing all night he did not feel in the least bit tired. And that was the tale that he told Margid when he got home, but she may not have believed him.

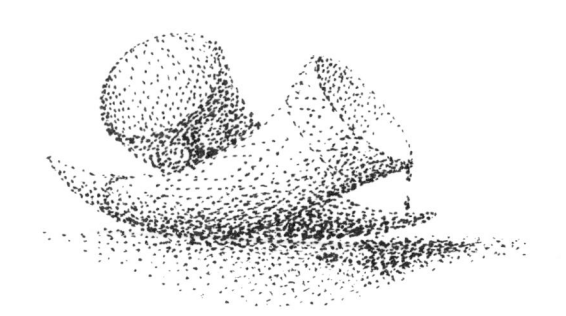

One day in winter when Tammy was working at the mill and there was snow on the ground there came a sudden thaw. The ice and snow on the hills melted and caused the burn to flood. When it was time to go home Tammy found that he was stranded on the wrong side of the burn. The wooden bridge he had to cross had been swept away and there were no other bridges over the burn. The only thing to do was to wade through the water, but it was too high and too strong for Tammy. But wade he must, and when he got home his clothes were as dry as a bone. Margid asked him how he had managed to cross the burn and still remain dry. He said that the fairies had carried him over the burn, and he stuck to that story until his dying day.

Tammy did get a fright with the fairies one day though. He was up in the hill cutting peats when down came a thick mist. Tammy headed for home, or at least where he thought home should be, for the mist was as thick as porridge. He had no idea where he was but he just chanced to luck. Suddenly Tammy found that he was not alone. There were fairies all around him, in front of him, behind him and on both sides of him. He found that it was no use to try and run. for the fairies had surrounded him. He didn't know what to do, but he took out his knife and stuck it into the fairy that stood before him. It neither cried out nor fell down, and Tammy took to his heels and ran all the way home, leaving his knife sticking in the fairy. How he found his way home is not known, but he made it somehow.

A week or two after that, one of Tammy's neighbours was working in the hill. The peats had been set up in small mounds to dry, and they were now ready to cart home. The man noticed something unusual and went over to see what it was. It was Tammy's knife, sticking out of one of the small mounds of peats.

The Nuckelavee

A man from Sanday called Tammy was out and about late one night, and though it was moonless it was a fine starlit night. The road that Tammy was on lay close to the sea, with a freshwater loch on the other side. Away in the distance he could see something moving. As it got nearer, Tammy could make out a huge black shape of a beast, the like of which he had never seen before. The thought that this must be some sort of supernatural creature dawned on Tammy, and a chill ran through his veins.

Now here was a fine predicament. There was water on both sides of him, and to turn your back on such creatures was the most dangerous act of all. He thought to himself: "The Lord be about me and take care of me, as I'm out with no evil intent tonight!" He decided to carry on walking, for he had a reputation of being a foolhardy sort of man.

As the creature got nearer he found to his horror that this was no other monster than the dreaded Nuckelavee, the most evil of all the uncannie beasts. The lower part of the monster was like a great horse, with fleshy fins that flapped around its front legs. The horse's mouth was as wide as that of a whale, and its breath billowed out like steam from a boiling kettle. It had but one eye, right in the middle of its head, and that eye glowed red like a burning coal. On this creature sat, or grew from out of its back as it seemed to Tammy, a huge man. He seemed to have no legs, but his arms were so long that they nearly reached the ground. His head was as big as a clew of simmans[1], and that is about three feet across, and seemed too heavy for his neck to support for the head rolled to and fro. But the thing that frightened Tammy most of all was that the monster had no skin on its naked body. He could see the monster's black blood

---

[1] A home made rope, usually made from twisted straw.

flow through its yellow coloured veins. As it moved Tammy could see white sinews as thick as horse tethers. stretch and twist.

Tammy went on in mortal terror not knowing what to do next. His hair was standing on end, there was a feeling like a sheet of ice under his scalp, and a cold sweat ran from every pore. He knew that there was no point trying to run, and he thought that if he must die he wanted to look his killer in the face. It was then that Tammy remembered that the Nuckelavee could not stand fresh water, so he walked close to the loch. The monster was moving in closer, and Tammy had no idea what to do to save his skin. As the lower head of the Nuckelavee came up to Tammy, it yawned like a bottomless pit. He could feel its hot breath on his face as the rider stretched out its long arms to grab him. Tammy swerved to try to avoid the monster's clutches, and as he did so he stumbled into the loch. Some fresh water splashed onto the horse's front legs and it gave a snort like a clap of thunder. It shied away in pain and Tammy could feel the wind of the Nuckelavee's fist as it swept past him.

Tammy saw his chance and he ran for his life. The Nuckelavee had turned and was now after him at full gallop and it bellowed with a sound like the roar of the sea. In front of Tammy was a small burn that ran from the loch down to the sea. He knew that if he could cross the running water then the Nuckelavee could not follow him. He strained every nerve in his body and made one desperate spring for the burn. He managed to jump clean across the fast flowing fresh water Just as the Nuckelavee tried to grab him. He felt the wind from its great hand again, closer than ever this time as the monster was left with Tammy's bonnet in its clutches. The Nuckelavee gave a wild scream of disappointed rage as Tammy fell senseless to the ground. safe on the other side of the burn.

The Fairies and the Vikings

A long time ago the Vikings left their homes in Norway and crossed the wide sea to the broken isles of Orkney. They sailed around the islands until they came to Rousay. There they saw a host of fairies standing on the hillside above Trumland. The sun glinted on their glittering spears so that it made a great impression on the Vikings. They turned their ship away from the shore and left. They did not stay away for long though, but returned to fight the fairies. The battle raged until the fairies were defeated and driven from their homes. They moved to the west side of the island and made new homes for themselves underground, and who knows, they may still be there.

The Bride of Ramray

A great excitement swept the island of Graemsay, for there was to be a wedding at Ramray. The barn was swept clean for the dancing and all sorts of lovely food was prepared for the feast. Young Jamie, the groom, was feeling very pleased with himself for his wife to be was Kitty Yorston, a bonnie lass with a wealthy father.

The great day dawned and the happy couple set off on their wedding walk with the rest of the island in attendance. After they were married the minister kissed the bride as was the custom, and led the dancing. The happy couple then returned to the house of Ramray for the festivities.

Now there was only one cloud on the horizon for Jamie and Kitty, and that was the selkie folk. Selkie men can take human form, and they liked to carry off human brides on their wedding night leaving in their place a sea wife. Their powers were limited though, they had to strike before sunrise on the wedding night itself. To protect the bride from this fate two young men were employed in walking around the house, keeping a close watch for unwelcome guests. The groom had his part to play too. He had to keep his right arm around his new wife and place his left hand over her heart. He was also to kiss her every now and again to help to weaken the selkie folk's spell.

While the merriment was going full swing inside, the two young men outside were keeping up their vigil. They walked around the house, looking and listening for any signs of a selkie man. When they turned the corner of the house what should they see but a large selkie at the mouth of the close. They ran up the narrow passage and grabbed the selkie. They tied its forepaws together with rope and then they dragged it to the end of the house. An iron pin was driven into the gable of the house and the selkie was hung from it, head downwards. One of the men then took his gully[1] and slit the selkie's throat. That was the end of him they thought, and they went in to tell the wedding party the good news.

With the selkie man out of the way the wedding went on livelier than ever. Kitty felt that it was now safe to mix with her friends, both inside and outside of the house. She urged her unmarried friends to look for a husband, for there was nothing like a wedding to turn people's thoughts to love. Jamie didn't have to kiss and cuddle his bride the whole time either, and he went on his rounds with an ale cog in his hand. But the sun had not yet risen above the horizon.

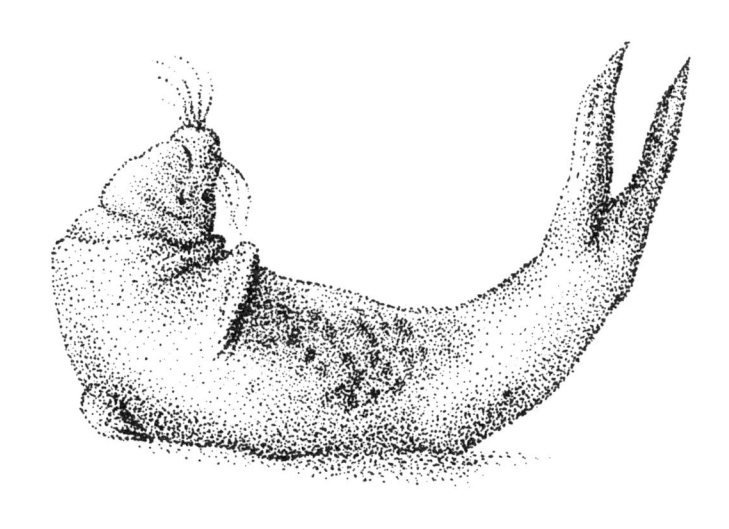

The revellers inside could hear a commotion, and when they ran outside Kitty Yorston was gone. In her place was a poor, weak sour thing, called a sea wife. They ran to the end of the house but the big selkie that had been hung there was gone. Now the wedding party broke up and the people went home with heavy hearts. Jamie's mother rounded on the poor man, telling him that he could never do anything right and that now he had lost his wife and all the dowry that went with her. He was to get 30 ells of blanket cloth, two pigs that were running in the Hoy Hills, a number of grey sheep, a young cow and a dozen beesmilk cheeses[2]. If they had sons they would have inherited all old Yorston's land, for he had no sons of his own. Jamie's lack of wit was put down to the fact that when he was born there was no silver spoon in the house to give him his first drink from, so they had to shove in a wooden one instead.

Jamie lived with his sea wife and they raised a large family. She was not as good a wife as Kitty would have been, but Jamie thought it wise to make do with what he had got.

[1] *A large knife.*
[2] *A type of cheese made by baking the first milk from a cow that has just calved.*

The Trow's Curse

There was once a farmer who had a large mound in one of his fields, believed to be a broch. The farmer decided that he would open the mound and see what was inside. He set to work digging into the mound, turning up middens filled with ash, bone and shells. At last he found a structure inside the mound, with small underground cells opening from the main room.

One summer's day the farmer was busy clearing out part of the building when something caught his eye. Before him stood an old grey whiskered man, dressed all in grey. His clothes were old and tattered and were patched in many places, and in his hand he clutched a bonnet. On his feet he wore an old pair of shoes made out of horse or cowhide, which were tied up with strips of skin. When he had the farmer's attention he began to speak.

"Well, Mr. ————, thou are working thy own ruin, believe me fellow, for if thou does any more work, thou will regret it when it is too late. Take me word, fellow, drop working in my house, for if thou doesn't, mark my word, fellow, if thou takes another shovelful, mark me words thou will have six of the cattle dying in thy cornyard at one time. And if thou goes on doing any more work, fellow - mark me word, fellow, thou will have then six funerals from the house. fellow; does thou mark me words; good-day, fellow." And with that he vanished.

The farmer scrambled out of the mound, trying to see where the strange old man had gone. He was nowhere to be seen, and the farmer never saw him again. The farmer went to see a neighbour of his for advice. The neighbour was a man who was known for his good judgement, and he advised him to wait and see what happened. Sure enough, the farmer lost six cattle in his cornyard all at the same time. Sadly, the prophecy of the six deaths in the house also came true as well.

Peerie Fool

There was once a king and queen who lived with their three daughters on the island of Rousay. The king died, and the queen lived with the princesses in a small house. They had a kailyard and a cow who gave them milk. One day the queen found that someone had been stealing their kail from the yard. The oldest daughter said that she would catch the thief, so she took a blanket and sat in the kailyard all night.

After a time what should she see but a huge great giant coming striding into the kailyard. He cut the kail and threw it into a caisie[1] on his back. As he filled his caisie the princess was always asking him why he was taking her mother's kail. The giant just replied that if she would not be quiet he would take her too. and so it was. When the giant had filled his caisie he took the princess by the arm and leg and threw her in the caisie on top of the kail and off home he went.

When they arrived at the giant's house he set her down and told her what work she had to do. First she must milk the cow, then put her up to the hills called Bloodfield. Then she had to take wool, wash it, tease it, comb it, card it, spin it and make it into cloth.

The giant left her to get on with her work. She milked the cow and put her up to the hills then she put on a pot to make some porridge for her breakfast. As she sat down to sup her porridge she found that she was not alone. A horde of little-yellow headed folk came running in, and they all begged her for some of her porridge, but this she refused, saying:

"Little for one, and less for two,
And never a grain have I for you."

[1] *A straw basket carried on the back.*

When she took up the wool she found that, try as she liked, it would not work for her. When the giant returned he found that she had not done her work. He took her, and starting with her head he pulled all her skin off down her back and over her heels. He then threw her body over the rafters among the hens.

That night the giant took his caisie and off he went to the Queen's kailyard again. When he got there who should he meet but the second princess. As he cut the kail she kept on asking him why he was stealing her mother's property. He warned her that if she didn't hold her tongue he would take her too. When the caisie was full he picked up the princess and tossed her on top and off home he went.

He gave the second princess the same tasks as he had given her sister. She milked the cow and put her to the hills, then put on her pot of porridge. The same little yellow-headed people came running in begging for a share, but they got the same answer:

"Little for one, and less for two,
And never a grain have I for you."

If the wool hadn't worked for her sister, it worked even worse for her. When the giant came home he found the work had not been done. He took the princess and tore a strip of skin from her head down her back and over her heels. He threw her over the rafters alongside her sister and the hens.

The next night the youngest princess said she would take a blanket and spend the night in the kailyard. She would find out who the thief was who was stealing the kail, and her sisters. Before too long the giant arrived and started to cut the kail. The youngest princess asked him why he was stealing her mother's kail, but the giant would only say that he would take her too if she wasn't quiet, and so he did. He picked her up by the arm and leg and tossed her in the caisie.

At the giant's house he gave her the same orders as he had given her sisters, and off he went. She milked the cow and put it to the hills, then she put on a pot of porridge. Again the little yellow-headed folk came running in begging some food. She was a kind girl and told them to go and get something to sup with, and so they did. Some took heather

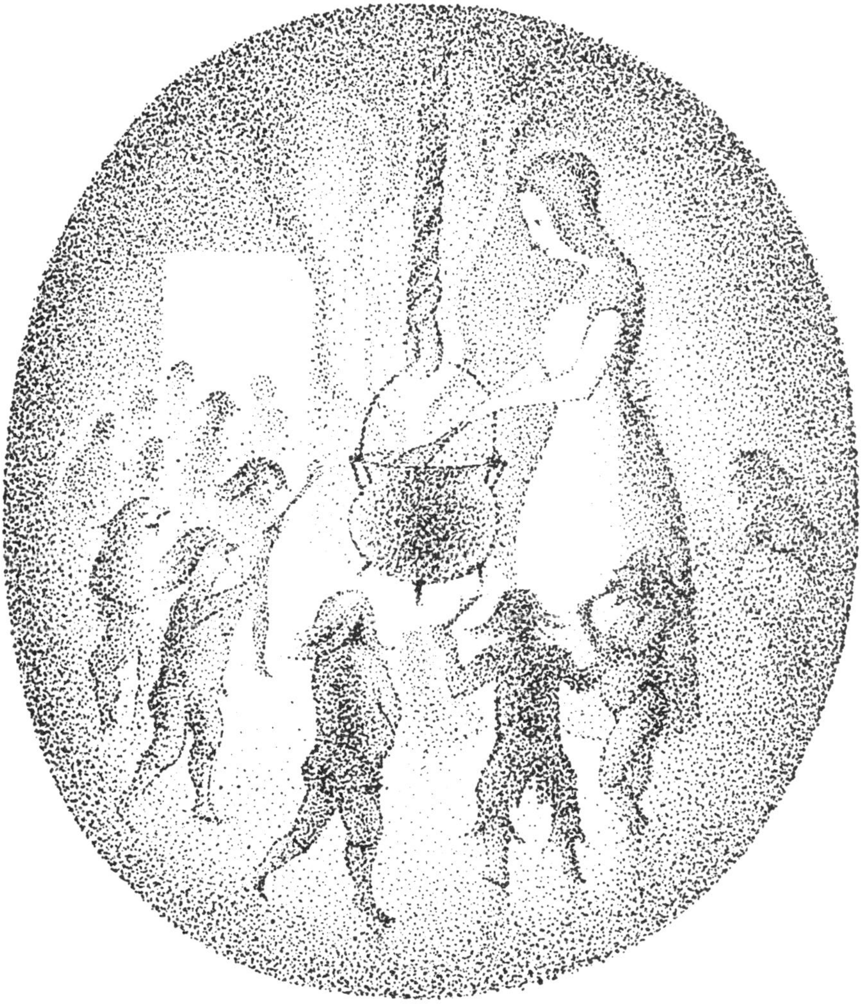

stalks, some took bits of broken dishes, some got one thing and some another. They supped the porridge until it was all done. After they had left a little yellow-headed boy came in and asked her if she had any work to do, he could do any work with wool. She said that she had a lot of work to do, but she could not pay him. He said that all he asked for was that she should tell him his name when he had finished. She agreed, thinking that it should be easy enough, so she gave him the wool.

When it was getting dark an old woman came asking for a bed for the night. The princess said that she could not put her up for the night, but asked her if she had any news. The old woman said she had none and went off to sleep outside.

There was a knowe near to the giant's home and the old woman took shelter under its lee side. She lay down on the side of its slope and found it to be very warm. As she lay on the knowe she was always climbing a little way up it until she found herself at its top. She thought she could hear a voice coming from inside the knowe, so she listened. The voice said: "Tease, teasers, tease; card, carders, card; spin, spinners, spin: for Peerie Fool, Peerie Fool is my name." There was a crack in the top of the knowe and the old woman peered inside. There were a great number of little people working, and a little yellow-headed boy running around them repeating that rhyme.

The old woman now thought that she had news that might win her a nights lodgings after all. She headed back to the giant's house and told the princess all that she had seen and heard. The princess kept on saying "Peerie Fool, Peerie Fool," over and over to herself. At last the little yellow-headed boy came in with the cloth. He asked her what his name was, and she made a few wrong guesses. Every time she guessed wrong, the tiny yellow headed boy would jump about shouting "No!" At last she said: "Peerie Fool is your name!" He threw down the cloth in a perfect rage and ran out of the house.

When the giant came home he met a great many little yellow-headed folk, and they were a terrible sight! Some had their eyes hanging out on their cheeks, some had their tongues hanging down to their breasts. He asked them what was the matter, how had they ended up like that. They said it was with working so hard pulling wool so fine. The giant said that if his own goodwife at home was alright he would never make her do any work again. When he came home he was very relieved to find her well, and stunned to see all the webs of cloth that she had made. The giant was as good as his word and the princess had no more work to do. In fact, he was very kind to her.

The next day the princess found her sisters and took them down from over the rafters. She put the skin on their backs again, and they were as good as new. She set her oldest sister in the caisie with some of the giant's fine things on top of her and covered it all over with grass. When the giant came home she asked him to take the caisie to her mother, saying it was food for her cow. The giant did as she wished, for he was fond of her now.

The next day she did the same thing with her other sister. The giant again set off with her in the caisie, along with other fine things from his home. When he got home the princess told him that she would have another caisie of grass for her mother's cow ready for him the following night. She would not be at home though, as she wanted to go somewhere. The next night the caisie containing the youngest princess and all the other fine things that she could find in the giant's house was left by the door for him. He could not see any of this, as it was covered over with grass. The giant picked it up and set out with it to the queen's house. When he got there the queen and her two daughters were waiting for him with a big boiler full of boiling water. When he was under the window they poured it over him, and that was the end of the giant.

The Trow Wife

There was once a peedie[1] boy called Johnny who lived in the island of Rousay. His home was a type of house called a "twa built hoose", that is two long houses with byres and barns at the ends. The boy used to go from one house to the other every night. One night he did not come in as usual. Time passed, but he never arrived. At last he was sent for, but there was no sign of him. A search followed, his family called to him: "Johnny boy, what's become of you?" After a while they heard him cry: "I'm on the back of the trow". The old trow woman who was carrying him off dropped him when she heard the word "trow" mentioned, for she had lost her powers. She turned and gave him such a clout on the crown of his head that it took all the hair off him, and he was bald for the rest of his days.

[1] *Small, little.*

Ursilla and the Selkie Man

There was once a woman who lived in the North Isles. She was a laird's daughter, and her father owned a lot of land and was a powerful man in the islands. She was a pretty woman, though she had a very stern manner and had to get her own way.

Now Ursilla thought that it was time that she took herself a husband. She was not the sort of person to wait though, and if anyone had come after her she would have sent them packing for their presumptuousness. Her eye fell on a handsome young man who worked as her father's barn-man. Ursilla knew that he would not do as a husband, for he was too far beneath her own class, but her love for him grew. She knew that if she told her father about her feelings, he would disinherit her on the spot and she would be left with not a penny to her name. So she kept her feelings to herself, locked away deep inside her heart. She treated the barn-man the same as the other servants, and he felt the sharp edge of her tongue many times.

Time passed, and her father died. Ursilla was now free to marry whoever she wanted for her fortune was secure. She went to the barn-man and ordered him to marry her. The poor man was too gallant to refuse her, and so they were wed. The wedding caused quite a stir among the gentry of Orkney. That one of their own class should marry a servant was unthinkable. Ursilla did not care what they thought. She made a good wife and ran things well. She kept the house in fine order, as well as ordering the running of the farm, and her husband.

Now everything seemed to be going well. She seemed happy with her husband and the farm, but this was only a show for the outside world. Ursilla was very disappointed with her choice of husband, for there was no love in their marriage. But she was too proud to admit it. She knew that the gentry would only say: "She shaped her own cloth, now let her wear her ill-fitting dress!", and that would have pleased them immensely. Her days were lonely, and so were the long dark winter nights. Not being the sort of person who sits and cries over their misfortunes, she decided to take a selkie lover.

 Early one morning she went and sat on the rocks at high water mark. When the tide was at its highest she cried seven tears into the sea. People said they were the only tears that she ever shed. But she knew that this was what you had to do if you wanted to talk with the selkie folk. The first light of dawn turned the water grey, and Ursilla saw something out in the sea. A big selkie was swimming towards the rock where she sat. He raised his head out of the water and spoke to her, saying: "What's your will with me, fair lady?" She told him her troubles, and what was on her mind. The selkie told her that he would meet her at the seventh stream[1], for that was when he could take human form.

 When the time came Ursilla met with the selkie man. They met again and again, and Ursilla found the company that she had been missing. When Ursilla's bairns were born, they all had webs between their toes and fingers, like the paws of a selkie, and did that not tell a tale. The midwife took scissors and clipped the webs, but they just grew back again. Ursilla clipped and clipped, but they kept growing back. Eventually, when the webs were not allowed to grow in their natural place they started to spread to the palms of the hands and the soles of the feet. They formed a horny crust known as "hard hands", still to be seen to this day on the descendants of Ursilla and her selkie man.

[1] *Spring-tide.*

The Dancers Under the Hill

One Hogmanay, a long, long time ago, two men were walking from Stromness back to their homes in Orphir. Their road took them past the farm of Howe where a great mound used to stand. One of them carried a pig[1] of whisky on his back, all ready for the New Year's celebrations.

As they passed the knowe of Howe they thought that they could hear the sound of fiddle music coming from inside it. They stood and listened for a time, then the man with the pig of whisky went a little nearer. He saw an open door in the side of the knowe, and out of it came some fairies. They persuaded him to come into the knowe with them and join in the fun. His friend sat down outside and waited for him to come out. After a while, with darkness closing in, and with no sign of his friend, the man went home alone.

A year later the same man was on his way home from Stromness and had to pass the knowe at Howe again. As he passed the knowe he heard the fiddle music again, so he went to have a closer look. He found the open door and peered inside. Who should he see dancing past him with not a care in the world, but his long lost friend. He still had the whisky pig on his back. The man in the knowe saw his friend outside, and called to him to join in the fun. "No, no, I'm not comin' in, but it's time you came out!" His friend gave a laugh and said: "Come in man, the fun's only just beginning." "Don't tell me that, you went in there a year ago, and just look at your boots!" The man's boots were in bits, with the soles worn away and the uppers all hanging about his ankles in tatters. The pig of whisky on his back was empty too.

[1] *A stoneware jar.*

How the Fin Folk lost Eynhallow

The lovely little island of Eynhallow lies between the island of Rousay and the Mainland. It was not always there though, but was won from the Fin Folk by magic. Here is the tale as it has been told for hundreds of years.

The goodman of Thorodale married a woman and they had three fine, strong sons. But trouble was lurking not too far away, for the wife died. The man was left with the three boys who had now grown up to be young men. Thorodale took himself another wife, and she was said to be the bonniest lass in all the parish of Evie. Thorodale loved his new wife very much and they lived for a time in happiness. One fine day Thorodale and his bonnie young bride were down in the ebb gathering shellfish. Thorodale sat down on some rocks to tie the lace of his rivlin[1]. His back was to his wife, and she was close to the edge of the water. Thorodale heard a terrible scream which made him leap to his feet. He turned just in time to see a dark man dragging his wife towards a boat. Thorodale ran towards them, but it was too late. The Fin man had his wife in the boat, and as Thorodale waded through the water the man pulled the oars and shot across the water. Thorodale ran to his own boat, pushing it into the water, but by the time he had got it afloat the Fin man's boat was out of sight, sped on by his magic. Thorodale never saw his bonnie wife again, but he was not the sort of man to take such a blow lightly. He rolled up his breeches, took off his stockings, and went down on his knees below flood-mark and swore that, living or dead, he would take his revenge on the Fin Folk.

---

[1] *A type of shoe made from untanned hide.*

Many days and sleepless nights were spent deep in thought as Thorodale plotted how to avenge his loss. Try as he might, he could not think of a way to punish the Fin Folk. Then one day he went out in his boat to the fishing. He lay in the Sound between Rousay and the Mainland, there was no Eynhallow there in those days you see. As he lay there in the slack water he heard a woman singing. Thorodale recognised the voice at once, for it was that of his own dear wife. He could not see her, but he listened as she sang:

"Goodman, greet no more for me,
For me again you'll never see;
If you would have of vengeance joy,
Go ask the wise spae-wife of Hoy."

Thorodale headed to the shore as fast as he could row. He took his staff in his hand, put his silver in a stocking, and set off for the island of Hoy. He found the spae-wife, and told her his mission. She said that there was nothing that would hurt the Fin Folk more than to lose any part of Hilda-Land, their summer island homes. She taught him the spell that would let him see Hilda-Land, for it's usually hidden from human eyes. She also told him what to do when he did see it. Armed with this knowledge Thorodale returned home and waited.

For nine nights, when the moon was full, Thorodale travelled to the Odin Stone in Stenness. Nine times he went around the stone on his bare knees, then he looked through the hole in the stone and wished that he had the power to see Hilda-Land. On the ninth night he knew what he was to do. He went home. bought a large quantity of salt and filled his meal girnel with it. Next to the girnel he set three caisies[2], and he told his three sons to be ready to follow him when he gave the word.

One beautiful summer morning, just after the sun had risen, Thorodale went out and looked towards the sea. There in the middle of the Sound lay a pretty little island that had never been there before. He knew that if he took his eyes off it for one moment he would never see it again. He wasted no time, but shouted to his sons: "Fill the caisies, and hold for the boat."

[2] *A type of straw basket carried on the back.*

The three sons ran to the boat, each one carrying a caisie of salt on his back. They joined their father in the boat and pushed her out to sea. Thorodale never once took his eyes off of the island, for he was the only one who could see it.

Suddenly, the boat was surrounded by a school of whales. The sons wanted to set after them and drive then onto the shore. but Thorodale knew better. They were only a magic trick of the Fin Folk to try and distract the men from their mission. Thorodale cried: "Pull for bare life! and the Devil drook[3] the delayer!" A giant whale lay between the boat and the island and it slowly turned and headed towards the boat. It opened its huge mouth so the young men thought that it would swallow the boat, and them with it. Thorodale, who was standing in the bow of the boat, thrust both hands into the nearest caisie and scooped up the salt. He threw it into the monster's gaping mouth and it disappeared in an instant, for it was only a trick of the Fin Folk.

As the boat headed for the shores of Hilda-Land, two beautiful mermaids stood singing. They were naked from head to waist and their golden hair floated around their snow white skin like dancing sunbeams. The song that they sang was so lovely that it went to the hearts of the rowers, and they started to slow down. Thorodale gave the two sons nearest to him a hard kick on their backs, saying to the mermaids: "Begone, you unholy limmers; here's your warning." and he threw crosses made from dried tangles[4] at the mermaids. They screamed, and sprang into the sea.

At last the boat touched the beach of Hilda-Land and Thorodale leapt out. There in front of him stood a terrible monster. It had tusks as long as a man's arm and feet as broad as quern stones. The monster's eyes blazed in its head, and it spat fire from its mouth. Thorodale took a handful of salt and threw it at the monster, hitting it right between the eyes. It disappeared, giving a terrible growl as it did so.

Then there stood in front of Thorodale a mighty man, tall and dark with hate in his eyes. In his hand he held a sword, and he roared out a challenge. "Go back, you human thieves, that come to rob the Fin Folk's land! Begone! or, by my father's head, I'll defile Hilda-Land with your

---

[3] *Drench.*
[4] *Kelp stem.*

nasty blood!" His speech frightened the sons, who called out: "Come home, Dad, come home!" The big Fin man made a thrust at Thorodale's breast with his sword, but Thorodale was too quick for him. He sprang to one side and threw a cross at the Fin man. The cross was made out of a kind of sticky grass known as cloggirs, twisted together. It stuck to the Fin man's face and he roared with pain. The Fin Folk are heathen, and cannot bear the sight or touch of the cross. Unable to brush it away, the Fin man ran off roaring in pain and anger. Thorodale smiled, he had seen that Fin man before; he was the one who had stolen his wife.

He shouted to his sons who were sitting in the boat, amazed by what they saw. "Come out of that, you duffers! and take the salt ashore!" The sons went ashore, each one carrying his caisie of salt. Then their father made them walk abreast around the island, scattering salt as they went. When they began to sow the salt there arose a terrible noise and commotion throughout the island. the Fin Folk and their cattle all ran helter-skelter to the sea like a flock of sheep with a score of mad dogs behind them. The men roared, the mermaids screamed and the cattle bellowed like it was the end of the world. It was awful to hear them. At last every soul and mother-son of them, and every hair of their cattle had taken to the sea, leaving only the four men to carry out their task.

As the rings of salt were growing around the island Thorodale took out a knife and cut nine crosses in the turf of the island. The three sons had sown three rings each around the island, making nine rings of salt in all. Well almost nine rings, for you see the youngest son had large hands and he ran out of salt before he had finished his last ring. He asked his brothers for salt to finish it, but they said that they had none to spare. So the last ring of salt was never finished, and that is why Eynhallow is still a magical place. No rats, cats or mice can live on the island. No iron stakes will remain in the ground after sunset. They jump right out, freeing any cattle, sheep or horses that are tethered there. They say that if you cut corn after the sun has gone down on Eynhallow the stalks will bleed.

That was the story of how the Fin Folk lost part of Hilda-Land. The island was called Hyn-hallow, for it was the hinmost holy, that is, the last island to be made holy. And that is all that I can tell you about it.

The Midnight Ride

Late one night a family in Sandwick were wakened by a loud banging on the house door. A voice was crying. "For God's sake, boys, let me in!" The young men of the house jumped out of their beds and ran to the door. When they opened it they found a man with a face as white as a sheet and shaking limbs. He was taken in, but it was a while before he could tell his story.

He had been out visiting friends in Birsay and had stayed out rather late. He had forgotten that his road home took him over the lonely hill road that led to Sandwick. It was not the sort of place that you should go after dark.

He left his friends house and started his long walk home. He reached the hill road, and all went well for a start. When he reached the top of the Sandwick Hill he saw to his horror that the fairies were out on their midnight ride. Right across his path they rode, fast and furious. The horses ran nose to tail and there was no way through for the terrified traveller. He stood trembling on the road waiting for a break in the procession. He then remembered that the word of God and cold steel were a good protection against the fairy folk. He took out his pocket knife and shouted in as loud a voice as he could manage: "In the name of the Lord let me through!"

The next moment he was standing alone on the road, and not a fairy in sight. He ran like his life depended on it. He told the youths who had let him into their home: "Oh, boys. I tell you I ran as I never ran in my life before, and I was always thought brave and swack[1].

The two lads accompanied him back to his house. It lay about half-a-mile away. He would not let them leave before he was in through his own door. He vowed that he would never, never cross the Sandwick Hill at midnight again.

[1] *Agile, supple.*

The Selkie Wife of Westness

The farmer of Westness in North Ronaldsay was a well-off and good-looking man. Many a young woman had tried to win his affections, but with no success. He seemed to think women were bad luck, and the lasses called him "an old young man". He was not interested in women, and when his friends told him that he should be looking for a wife he would dryly reply: "Women are like many other things in this weary world, only sent as a trial to man; and I have trials enough without being tried by a wife. If that old fool Adam had not been bewitched by his wife, he might have been a happy man in the yard of Eden to this day." The old woman of Longer heard that speech, and her blood boiled. She said: "Take care of yourself, you'll maybe be bewitched yourself some day." "Aye" he replied, "that will be the day when you walk dry shod from the Alters o' Seenie[1] to the Boar of Papey."

One day the goodman of Westness was down on the shore when he saw a number of selkie folk on a flat rock nearby. Some were sunning themselves, others were jumping around and playing. They were all naked, and their skins were as white as his own. Their cast off seal skins were lying near to where they played. On one side of the flat rock was deep blue water while on the other side was a shallow pool. The man crept towards the pool without being seen. He then sprang to his feet and ran through the pool towards the selkie folk. They grabbed their skins and splashed into the sea, alarmed at being disturbed. If the selkie folk were fast the man was as quick, for he snatched one of the seal skins. All the selkie folk took to the water, back in seal form. All except one. As he walked up the beach he heard sobbing coming from behind

---

[1] *Probably the Alters of Linay.*

him. He turned to see a lovely young selkie woman following him. She was sobbing like her heart was breaking.

As the big tears rolled down her face she begged: "Oh, bonnie man! If there's any mercy in your human breast, give me back my skin! I cannot, cannot live in the sea without it. I cannot, cannot, cannot live among my own folk without my own seal skin. Oh, pity a poor distressed, forlorn lass, if you would ever hope for mercy yourself!"

The man had a hard heart, but he could not help pity the young woman that stood before him. With pity came love, for the selkie lass was very beautiful. He had never felt that way before, but he was unable to fight it. He refused to give her back her skin, but wanted her to come home with him and become his wife. She cried many tears before she was forced to agree to the man's wishes. She had no option, as she could not live in the sea without the skin. So she went with him and became his wife, and she was a loving wife, good at housework and cooking.

She bore the man of Westness seven children, four boys and three girls. There were no bonnier bairns in all the island than the ones at Westness. They lived together happily for many years and things went well at the farm. But sometimes she looked sad, like there was a great weight on her heart. She would spend hours staring out to sea with a faraway look on her face. She taught her bairns many strange songs that nobody had ever heard before. The goodman led a happy life with his selkie wife, but she was a thing of the sea and longed to return.

One day the man took his three eldest sons off in the boat to the fishing with him. The wife sent three of the others off to the ebb to gather limpets and welks. The youngest bairn, a girl, was at home with her mother. She had a cut on her foot that had become poisoned, and she sat on a stool with her foot up. Her mother started to clean the house from top to bottom, or at least that was what she told the bairn. She was really looking for her missing skin, and now was a good time to do it.

She hunted high and low until the little girl asked: "Mam, what are you looking for?" Her mother said, "Oh, bairn, don't tell, but I'm looking for a bonnie skin to make a rivlin[2] that would cure your sore foot." The

---

[2] *A type of shoe made from untanned hide.*

lass smiled: "Maybe I know where it is," she said. "One day, when you were out, and dad thought I was sleeping in the bed, he took down a bonnie skin, he stared at it for a peedie[3] minute, then folded it and laid it up under the aisins[4] above the bed."

[3] *Little, small.*
[4] *The space between the first row of flagstones and the top of the wall.*

When her mother heard this she ran over to the bed, looked under the roof space, and pulled out her long-lost skin. She turned to her daughter saying: "Farewell, peedie buddo[5]!" and then ran out of the door. She rushed down to the shore, flung on her skin, and plunged into the sea with a wild cry of delight. A large male selkie swam to meet her, and they greeted each other joyfully. At that moment the goodman of Westness came rowing up in his boat. The selkie wife uncovered her face to speak to him. "Goodman o' Westness, farewell to thee! I liked you well, you were good to me, but I loved better my man of the sea." She covered her face and the two selkies dived out of sight. She was never seen again. The man of Westness often wandered the shore, looking for his lost wife, but she never came back. He kept up his silent vigil, but he was never to see her bonnie face again.

[5] *A term of endearment.*

The Farmer and the Trow Servant

There was once a farmer on the Mainland who had a very strange servant. It was a trow who did all sorts of odd jobs around the farm. For all its work the trow never received anything more than a morsel of food.

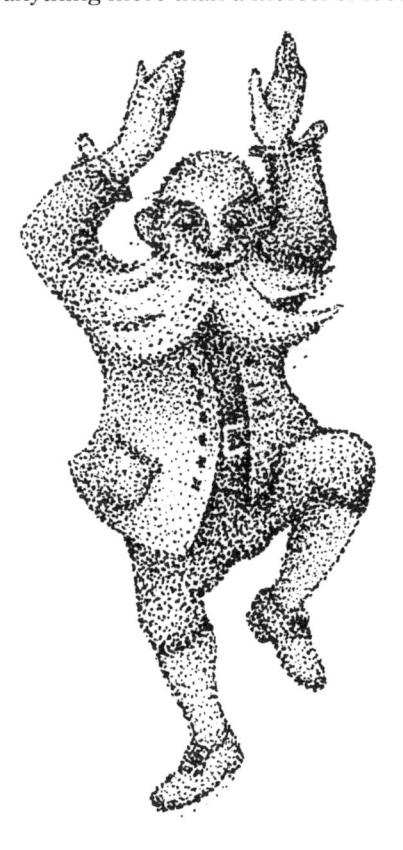

Now the farmer took a wife, and a bonnie lass she was too. She was not a country lass though, she came from the town of Kirkwall. She did not seem to be in any way frightened by the trow as he worked quietly around the farm. Winter rolled around, and with it the cold icy winds that whistle down from the north. The farmer's wife felt sorry for the trow as he had hardly any clothes, and the ones he did have were hanging in rags. She decided that she would make the trow a new set of clothes to keep out the winter chill. She made a jacket, trousers, and even managed to get a pair of shoes that would fit him. She left her gifts out for the trow that night and went to bed, happy with her good deed.

Later that night the farmer and his wife were wakened by loud shouts coming from the kitchen. They recognised the shouts as being those of the trow, so they went to investigate. When they entered the kitchen, there was the trow in his fine new suit of clothes. The trow laughed at them and shouted: "I'm a gentleman now! I'm far too good to work for the likes of you!" and off he went. Neither the farmer nor his wife ever saw him again. The farmer complained long to his wife about her kind act. He said that if she had not made him his new clothes the trow would still be working for them.

The Man from Nowhere

A Stronsay farmer was having a run of bad luck. The farm was not doing well and every kind of misfortune had occurred. One day a strange young man arrived on the farm looking for work. No-one had seen the youth before, and they asked him many questions about who he was and where he was from. The young man avoided answering any of the questions put to him. In the end the old woman of the house said: "Leave him alone, and be good to him." She was a wise old woman. and so they all welcomed the stranger to the farm. All that is except one.

Now the farmer's luck began to change and everything was going well. The stranger was a very good worker, and was popular with the farmer and his men. He only asked for one thing, though it was a very strange thing to ask for. He wanted to eat all his meals in private, and so the farmer agreed. The youth asked for more food, saying that what he got was not enough. The farmer complied with his request. He was a good worker and seemed to have brought some much needed luck to the farm.

One night some of the farm servants began to talk about why the stranger wanted to eat his meals alone. They went to the young man's room and peeped in. He was eating his meal, but every now and again he would pass some of the food over his shoulder. The food would disappear, like it was being snatched by a person or persons unseen. The men suspected that the youth was in league with the fairies.

One day after a very successful fishing trip, a group of islanders had gathered to haul up the boat. They soon found that it was too heavy to move no matter how hard they pulled at it. It was finally decided to send one of their number to get more men to help pull up the boat. The stranger stepped forward saying that he could pull up the boat, but all the men had to leave him alone to do it. They all agreed, and started to walk up the beach. They had not gone far when the youth shouted to them: "Go down and shore your boat, boys." The boat was back in its noust safe and sound.

There was one member of the farm that did not like the strange young man. This was a useless lout of a farm servant, and he neither thought that the lad was useful nor indeed had any connections with the fairies. He treated the youth badly whenever he had the chance. One moonlit night the useless farm servant was on his way home from courting a local girl. As he walked along the road he received a wallop on the side of the head which knocked him into the ditch. When he stood up to see who had hit him he received another blow to the other side of his head. He was then kicked and punched from all sides, but he could not see a living soul to fight back against.There seemed to be too many for one man to fight anyway. He took to his heels and ran back to the farm, but the kicks and punches continued all the way. He burst in through the kitchen door, more dead than alive. The people were shocked to see him in such a state. He told them about the attack that he had suffered, and they were all amazed. But the man from nowhere smiled a knowing and malicious smile.

This may have been the settling of an outstanding account, for the strange young man disappeared one morning soon after. The farmer found he had gone as suddenly and mysteriously as he had arrived. He was never seen again. The loutish servant recovered from his ordeal, hopefully a better and wiser man. The farmer's luck changed for the better, and the shadow of misfortune never fell across his threshold again.

The Dead Wife with the Fairies

There was a young couple in North Ronaldsay who were newly married. All went well for a time and they were very happy. But the woman became ill, and died. The man was heart broken at the sudden loss of his young wife, and he wondered if there was anything that he could do about it.

He went to see an old woman who lived on the island and was said to be a witch. He told her his tale of woe, and she said that there was indeed something that he could do to see his wife again. Now at that time the lighthouse had not yet been built. On the site where it now stands stood a mound called the Brae o' Versabreck. The old woman told him to go there on the night of the full moon. He must bring with him a heavy oak staff, a bible and a black cat. At the base of the mound he would see something like a cave. He was to call his wife by name, then read a verse or two from a psalm in the bible, and lastly to throw in the black cat. He would see his wife rise up from this cave, but the fairy folk would try to stop her. He must grab his wife, while thrashing at the fairies with the staff. He would then be able to talk to his wife all night, but she had to return at daybreak.

The man did as he was told. On the night of the full moon he went to the mound, called his wife's name, read the bible. threw in the black cat and saw his wife rising from the mouth of the cave. The fairies tried to stop her, but he leapt in amongst them, threshing them with his staff. He then had the night to talk to his wife. He did this on every night of the full moon until the day he died.

The House on Sule Skerry

Two men from the North Dyke district of Sandwick took their boat from its noust in the Bay of Skaill and went to the fishing. After a few hours the wind began to rise and the boat was driven out to the wide open sea. They ran before the storm for the whole night, but as the day dawned they saw land. It was the small island of Sule Skerry that lies out in the Atlantic Ocean. They found a place where they could pull up their boat, and went ashore. They thought that they had better find a place to shelter until the storm passed.

They were very surprised to find a little house on the deserted island. They went up to the door and knocked. A young woman answered the door, and the two men recognised her at once. She was the Rowland lass who had disappeared some time before. She invited them in and asked for all the news from home. After they told her how things were with her family they asked her how she came to be living on the island, and she told them her tale.

She had been down on the shore of Leygabroo in the Bay of Skaill gathering bait. She had forgotten her father's warning, and turned her back to the sea. Suddenly, rough arms were around her and she was dragged away by a man from the sea. She was too frightened to say "God save me", which would have driven her attacker away, and he carried her to Sule Skerry. She said that it had turned out well, for he had made a good husband and she thought that she would not have got such a good man on land.

She then told them that they would see a seal coming in through the door, but to pay no attention to it. She also warned them not to ask her to go home with them, for her husband loved her very much and would not part with her. They agreed to her request, and they chatted away happily.

A short time later the door opened, and in came the seal. He went flittering through the house to the ben end. A quarter of an hour later. a fine big man in grand clothes came through from the ben-end and welcomed the two fishermen. He said that he was happy that their boat had survived the gale and that they were welcome to enjoy his hospitality. He asked his wife if supper was ready. and they all sat down to a lovely meal of fish.

The two fishermen told their hosts that they had never tasted such delicious fish in all their lives. The man laughed, saying that he had caught those fish from below the two men's own house of Unigarth. After their supper they retired to bed, and a sound night's sleep.

The new day dawned fine and clear, and the two men turned for home. They thanked the couple for all their kindness, and set sail back to Sandwick with news of the lass who was thought to be dead. When they got home they told all the North Dyke folk their wondrous story, and it has been handed down to generations of good believing folk ever since.

The Death of the Mainland Fairies

The fairies were finding life on the Mainland too tough for them. There had been an awful plague of ministers sweeping the land and you could not move for the sounds of prayers. Holy water was being fired about like rain in January. All these things were truly frightening to the fairies, who were in league with the Devil. They had a meeting and decided to move to Hoy as things were a bit better there. They would have more quiet open places to live in, away from ministers and hymn singing. So it was decided that they would go one night when the moon was full.

The moon rose as full and round as a clootie dumpling, and as bright as a silver dish. The fairies gathered at the Black Craig in Stromness parish, and took with them a simman[1] rope. The most agile fairy took one end of the rope and leapt clean across the sea to Hoy. He fastened his end securely for the rest to use as a bridge. The other end was made good and they all crept slowly across the simman rope. But when they were only halfway across, the rope broke and they all fell into the sea and were drowned. The solitary fairy on the other side wailed like a dog when he saw what had happened, and he threw himself into the sea and was carried away with the rest. And that was the end of the Mainland fairies.

---

[1] *A home made rope, usually made from twisted straw.*

The Mermaid Bride

Johnie Croy was the bravest and most handsome man in all the broken isles of Orkney. Many a maiden's heart would flutter at the sight of him, but in vain, for Johnie never showed the slightest interest in them.

One day Johnie went to the shore to look for driftwood. The tide was out, so he walked under the craigs on the west side of Sanday. As he picked his way between the boulders on the beach there came to his ears the most beautiful sound that he had ever heard. He stopped dead in his tracks and listened. A song so sweet that it made his head spin came dancing around him. His senses deserted him completely as the beautiful music filled both his head and his heart, so that Johnie thought he would burst.

He thought that the music seemed to be coming from around the corner of the craig, and he slowly edged closer and closer. At last he was able to peep around the side of the rock to see what could be making the beautiful sound. He eyes grew wide with wonder as he saw before him a mermaid. She was sitting on a seaweed covered rock, combing her long golden hair. It shone so brightly that the sun hid behind a cloud in shame. She was naked from her head to her waist, but the lower part of her body was clothed in a petticoat. It was silver in colour and glittered like the stars on a frosty night. The lower end of it was folded together and lay behind her like a tail. Her golden hair floated down over her white skin like sunshine playing about a pillar of snow.

This would have been a sight that would have frightened most men out of their wits, but not Johnie. He was a stranger to fear, and the more he saw her the more he wanted her. The hot fires of love burned strong in his brave heart. He went down on his knees and swore by the Meursteen[1] that he would court this maiden of the deep and win her for his wife, even if it cost him his life. All this time the mermaid sat combing her hair and singing. She had her back to the sea and Johnie could only see the side of her face, but that was enough to set his heart beating like thunder.

Although his head swam with love he still had some of his wits about him. Slowly he crept down among the boulders until he was between the mermaid and the sea. Every now and then he would cast a glance at her, and his heart would race. He crept up behind her without her knowing that anyone was there. She went on combing her hair and humming her lovely tune. When he was a few feet away from her he knew it was time to make his move. He sprang forward and flung his arms around her neck and kissed her sweet mouth over and over again. He had fallen deep under her spell, and he thought that he was in paradise.

For a moment the mermaid sat where she was, too shocked to move. Then she sprang to her feet and flung Johnie to the rocks and gave him a blow with her tail that made his spine jump. She opened the tails of her petticoat and ran for the sea as if all the devils in hell were behind her. Johnie staggered to his feet, cursing that it was the first time that anyone had laid him flat. As he looked at the sea he saw the mermaid staring at him with flaming eyes. They burned with anger, but they also had the flames of love flickering in them. A mixture of feelings leapt up in the sea maid's breast. She was angry that he had so rudely kissed her, but his kisses had left their mark. The warm embrace of humankind had filled her heart with love for Johnie.

As he stood there Johnie saw something glistening among the seaweed at his feet. It was the mermaid's golden comb. She had dropped it when she ran to the sea. Johnie held up the comb and cried: "Thanks to you, bonnie lass, for you've left me a love token." When she saw her comb she gave a bitter cry. "Aloor, aloor! Oh give me back my golden comb! To lose it is the sorest shame that could ever befall me. Aloor, aloor! Wherever I go the Fin Folk will call me the lass that lost her golden comb. Oh give me back my comb!"

Johnie kept his head and said: "No, my sweet bonnie buddo[2]. You'll

---
[1] *A stone on which oaths were sworn.*
[2] *A term of endearment.*

come and live on land with me, for I can never love another creature but your own lovely self."

"No. no," said the mermaid, "I couldn't live in your cold land. I couldn't stand your black rain and white snow. And your bright sun and reeky fires would wizen me up in a week. Come you with me, my bonnie, bonnie lad, and I'll make you a chief among the Fin Folk. I'll set you in a crystal palace, where sunbeams never blind, where winds never blow, and raindrops never fall. Oh, come away with me, bonnie man, and be my own loving marrow, and we'll both be as happy as the day's long."

"No, No! You needn't entice me." said Johnie; "I wasn't born yesterday. But, oh, my peedie[3] dove, come with me! I have a stately house at Volyar, with plenty of gear, plenty of cows and sheep. and you'll be mistress of them all. You'll never want for anything. Just come away and stay with me, my darling Gem-de-lovely."

They argued back and fore for some time, and as they talked they admired each other all the more. Eventually the mermaid saw some people in the distance, for the sea folk can see far. She bade him farewell, and swam away out to sea, singing: "Aloor, aloor! My golden comb." Johnie watched as her golden hair streamed over the water, like sunbeams dancing over white sea foam.

Johnie walked home, carrying the comb close to his heart. His eyes were downcast and the heart that had once felt as light as a butterfly now felt like a lump of lead in his breast. When he got home, Johnie told his mother all about the mermaid, and showed her the comb. The old woman was a wise woman, some said that she was a spae-wife. She shook her head and sighed: "You're a great fool! To fall in love with a sea lass, when there's plenty of your own kind that would be glad to have you. But men will be fools all the world over. So if you want to have dealings with her, you must keep her comb as the dearest treasure. While you have her comb, you'll have power over her. Now, if you're wise you'll take my advice and cast her comb into the sea, and think no more about the limmer, for I can tell you, though she may make your summer bright and bonnie, it'll end in a woesome winter. But I see you'll ride your own road, and sink in the quagmire at it's end."

[3] *Little, small.*

Johnie went about his work like a man in a trance. All day long he could think of nothing but his beautiful mermaid. He locked up the comb in a safe place, and waited.

One night Johnie could not sleep a wink. He tossed and turned, but it was no use. All he could think about was his Gem-de-lovely. As dawn approached he fell into a slumber, but as the first light of the day filtered into his little room he thought he heard music. As he drifted from out of his sleep, Johnie thought he could hear the song of his sea maid. Her beautiful song filled the room as Johnie lay still in his bed, spellbound. Slowly he came to his senses as he recognised the song and voice of the mermaid. He sat up with a start and saw Gem-de-lovely sitting at the foot of his bed. She was even more beautiful than he remembered, and she wore a dress more lovely than any that Johnie had ever seen before. He tried to say a prayer, but the words would not come to him

At last she spoke: "My bonnie man, I've come back to ask if you'll give me back my golden comb. I've come to see if you'll come with me and be my loving marrow."

"No," said Johnie, "my sweet bonnie buddo. You know I can't do that. But, my own bonnie darling, you will stay with me and be my own dear wife. Oh, Gem-de-lovely, if you leave me again my heart will break for love of you."

"I'll make you a fair offer." said the mermaid: "I'll be your marrow. I'll live with you here for seven years, if you'll swear to come with me, and all that's mine, to see my own folk at the end of the seven years."

Johnie jumped out of bed and fell on his knees before her. He swore by the Meursteen to keep his bargain. They fell into each others arms and kissed and cuddled as happy as the day is long.

The day came that they were married, and what a couple they made. The people of Sanday said that they had never seen such a beautiful bride. Her dress shone with silver and gold and around her neck was a string of pearls, and each one as big as a cockle shell. As the priest prayed Gem-de-lovely stuffed her hair in her ears to block out the sound, for the sea folk can't stand to hear the word of God.

Gem-de-lovely made Johnie a good and loving wife. She baked the best bread and brewed the strongest ale in all the island of Sanday. She was also the best spinner, and kept everything in the best of order. There was no better wife, or mother, than Gem-de-lovely. Every day was like Yuletime at Volyar. But it's a long day that has no end, and the seven years soon slipped by. Preparations were under way for the voyage, and as she worked Gem-de-lovely had a far away look in her eyes. Johnie had plenty to think about too, but he said nothing.

By this time Johnie and his wife had seven children, and bonnier bairns had never been seen before in all of Orkney. Each of the bairns had been weaned in Grannie's bosom, and now she had the youngest bairn sleeping with her in her own house. The night before the day of the journey, Johnie's mother made her plans. She banked up the fire until it burned brightly. At midnight she bent a piece of wire into the shape of a cross and put it on the fire. When it glowed red she took it from the fire and laid it on the bare backside of the bairn. He screamed like a demon.

The next morning dawned bonnie and fair. The boat was prepared, and Gem-de-lovely's people had come to help. She left Volyar and walked down to the boat. She was a sight to see. Her long golden hair shone in the sun and she wore her finest clothes. She was as stately looking and grand as a queen. She saw her husband and their six oldest children with him in the boat. She sent her servants up to Grannie's house for her youngest boy, but they returned empty handed. Try as they might, they said, they could not lift the cradle, even the four of them could not budge it an inch. A cloud passed over the mermaid's beautiful face and she ran up to the house. She tried to lift the cradle, but it would not move. She pulled back the blankets and tried to lift the child, but when her hand touched it a burning pain shot up her arm, and she jumped back with a wild scream. She walked back to the boat with her head hanging down and the salt tears running down her face. All the time Grannie sat on a rock with tears in her eyes. and a laugh hanging around her mouth. As the boat sailed away the mermaid was heard to sing a sad lament: "Aloor, aloor! for my bonnie bairn. Aloor for my bonnie boy. Aloor to think I must leave him to live and die on dry land." Away they sailed, nobody knows where, but Johnie Croy, his mermaid bride, and their six eldest bairns were never seen by mortal eyes again.

Grannie brought up the youngest boy, and named him Corsa Croy, that is Croy of the Cross. He grew up to be a terribly strong and handsome man. When his Grannie died he took to the sword, and went to fight in the holy land. He was a great warrior, and gathered a great store of wealth from the chiefs that he slew. He married a jarl's daughter, and they lived in the south country. They had many bairns and plenty of worldly gear. They lived happy, and if not dead they are living yet.

Appendices

A Hether Blether Story

There was a young woman from Yesnaby who disappeared. A long search proved unsuccessful, and it was thought that she had fallen into the sea and been carried away by the tide. A short time after this her brother went to sea, and made many successful voyages. Many years later his ship was driven by a storm towards a small island that they had never seen before. The crew went ashore and found a cottage, where they asked for help. On entering the house the men saw that the only person in the house was the skipper's long lost sister. Her brother asked her how she came to be there, but she would not say. She asked about the people of Yesnaby, but was always glancing out of the window that looked towards the shore. After a while she told the men that they would see a selkie come in through the door, but to pay no attention to it.

Not long after, the door opened and in came a fine looking selkie. It looked around at the men and then went through the house to the ben end. It wasn't long before a finely dressed man came through from the ben end and sat in a chair by the fire. The man asked about the people of Yesnaby and Skaill, and the surrounding areas. "You've had a severe storm." said the man, "but with my assistance you may be able to get safe home again." He then gave them his advice. They should stay on the island until the moon had waned, then he would give them a ball that they had to throw into the sea when they were a certain distance from land. "But you must be very careful," he said, "in every particular, else you will be driven back again." He also said that they would have a fair wind.

The fair wind came as the man said, and it was time to set sail. When they thought that they were at the exact place the ball was thrown over the side. The ship had only gone about twice its length when the wind changed and turned into a hurricane. The ship was tossed on the raging sea, and they eventually found themselves back in the bay of the island where they had started from. They returned to the house and were met by the selkie man at the door. "Well," he said, "fortune has not favoured you." "No," said the sailors, "what would be the reason?" "Ah!" said the man, "you had not arrived at the proper place; you threw over the ball too soon, and you did not pay sufficient attention to the marks I gave you. Indeed, I was not far away from you at the time and noticed all you did. You must be more exact next time."

The ship was got ready and sailed away for the second time, and all was well for quite a while. When they thought they were at the right spot the ball was thrown over the side, but with the same result. The ship was driven back to the island once more. For a third time they sailed, and the magic ball was thrown into the sea. This time it was at the right place and they had a good wind that took them home. The people of the district were amazed to hear their story. The skipper of the ship never saw his sister again, and who knows. she may be living with her selkie husband yet.

Original source, R. Menzies Fergusson, "Rambles in the Far North" 1884, 233-236.

Assipattie and the Stoorworm

There was once a farmer who had a son who would neither fight nor work. All he did was sit by the fire rakin through the ashes, so they called him Assipattie.

Now a terrible monster appeared in the sea near to the land where Assipattie lived. It was called the Stoorworm, and was so big that when it breathed in and out it caused the sea to ebb and flow. To keep the monster from destroying the land the people had to feed him with young maidens.

Assipattie's father told him that instead of lying by the fire all day he should try to rid the land of this terrible monster. Asipattie took a pot and put a burning peat in it. He carried it to the boat and set sail towards the Stoorworm. He sailed right down its mouth and a long way into the monster. He found the Stoorworm's liver and set it on fire with the burning peat. He then managed to escape out of the Stoorworm's mouth.

The fire in the Stoorworm's liver killed the monster. As it died some of is teeth fell out and made the islands of Orkney, Shetland and Faroes. It curled up into a lump and died, and its body made Iceland. Its liver is still on fire, and that is now Mount Hekla.

Version of the Stoorworm story told by Peter Leith, Langbigging, Stenness, by his mother Mrs Johina Leith.

The Master Whale

"An old man attributed the tides to be caused by a large fish which had its habitation in the Northern Ocean somewhere about the North Cape. This large fish he called the Maister Whal.

. . . He said this whal, or whale, lay somewhere about the Noth Cape; when he opened his mouth the water rushed in and caused the ebb and the continual set of the tide to the north . . . He then went on to state that when the maister whal shut his mouth then the water rushed out and so made the flood tide. Boy, I saw the Master Whale once. We had been to Archangel for tar and other things and coming around the North Cape he rises, and if you like to believe me – that was the difficulty – he was that high that what of him (that) was above the water took the sun out of sight of us for a whole week, and when he moved his tail the water all flew up like the merry dancers.[1] Our captain ordered all hands to set every stitch of sail on her, just as much as ever she (the ship) could stagger under, and it took us a whole week before we could get clear of his head; but such a mouth as he had."

[1] *The aurora borealis.*

This man was repeating the stories that he heard when a boy, and was merely keping them from rusting by fancying them taking place in his own experience."

George Marwick, in unpublished paper "Legends" 1903. Dialogue changed from Orkney dialect to English to aid understanding. Stromness Museum's archives, also copy amongst Ernest Marwick's papers in the Orkney Archives of the Orkney Library, D31/4.

Three North Ronaldsay Tales

At the beginning of the nineteenth century a North Ronaldsay woman had a child. The fairies came to hear about it and they put a 'shaun' on her (that is a spell). Her husband was told that she must never be left alone. They slept in a box-bed, and if the husband had to leave the house he nailed the doors of the bed closed so that she could not get out.

One day she did get out, and her family could not find her. A "wise woman" told them to go and look for her body. If it lay with its head towards the land then her soul was safe, and she would be in Heaven. If it lay with its head to the sea, then her soul was lost. They found her body on the rocks at Sava Geo. There were two white birds sitting on the dead woman's head, which was turned towards the land. The birds were a good omen, and meant that her soul was in Heaven.

Another woman on North Ronaldsay had a child, and the fairies had put a 'shaun' on her. Her husband was told to nail together the doors of the box-bed, and to fire a gun three times over the house. He did not nail the doors well enough, and when he had to leave her alone in the house she was taken. In her place the fairies had left a mad woman, called a 'stock'.

Long, long ago in North Ronaldsay there was a house standing in the north-west corner of the island. One day a fine looking bull came out of the sea and went with one of the cows from this house. A quey calf was born and it was a fine calf with beautiful sleek black hair. The hair on the calf was curly, but it curled up in the wrong direction.

The quey had many calves, and there was not another herd of cattle like them in all of Orkney. One night, many years later, a voice was heard calling from the sea. It said:

"Brak thee baund, Boro,
Tak wi' theee aull thee store-o."

The cow and all her offspring broke their bands and headed down to the sea. They went right in, and were never seen on land again.

Original source, Mary A. Scott, "Island Saga, The Story of North Ronaldsay". No publication date given, 156-157.

The Tinkler and the Trow

There was once a tinkler (tinker) called Old Mac. He used to go from island to island selling dishes. He told a story of when he was a young man on a visit to Hoy. He was in the district of Brims, and his road took him past a large mound. As he drew near the mound he saw the figure of a small dark man standing at a door in its side. The small man spoke to him, saying: "Boy! What are you selling?" "Dishes," Mac replied, "plates and bowls; cups and saucers, and faith boy, even a chanty[1] or two." "Come inside, boy", said the small man. The next thing that Mac knew he was standing in a large room inside of the mound. What happened next he was not sure, for it all happened so fast. the next that Mac knew he was back outside, sitting on top of the mound. His basket of dishes was empty, but in their place were five gold sovereigns. He looked around the mound but there was no sign of the door.

[1]*Chamber pot.*
Original source, John Bremner, "Hoy, The Dark Enchanted Isle" 1997, 94-95.

Short stories from Old Lore Miscellany

A midwife living in Evie had a visit from a strange man who asked for her help as his wife was in trouble. She agreed to go and the man blindfolded her and took her to a house that she did not recognise. She was treated very kindly, and stayed there until the child was born. When she saw that both mother and child were well she left. Once more she was blindfolded and led back to her house. All the people she saw were strangers, and she thought that they must be Fin men.

A woman in Westray had a child, and the fairies came to steal the mother away. She untied the ropes as fast as they could tie them, so they never got her. The reason they wanted her was that one of the fairies had died and they wanted her to nurse the fairy bairn.

Two men passing the knowe at Garth in Westray heard a dreadful cry, "Oh, come hame, Ailie's bairn has fa'en in the fire and brunt it." "Not hid. hid canna be mine, hid's ould Lawrie's bairn."

A man was standing on the side of Knock-ha' Hill, Westray, when he looked to the south and saw all the fairies riding on a tangle, and the people between them never saw them.

Duncan J. Robertson, "Orkney Folk-Lore Notes", Vol.II, pt.II 1909, 105-109.

Hodgeylay near Garth in Westray was famous for its fairies, who used to steal milk from the farm of Garth. One day a girl was passing the knowe when she heard the Stout Stumbler say that he had been burnt or bruised. She told this to another woman by the byre door when a fairy stumbled and another dashed out past them, in great distress at the news.

Vol II, pt.I 1909, 22-23. Original source George Petrie's notebook no. 9 1866, 135.

There was a click mill at Hillside. Birsay, called the Mill of Skeldie. The miller was called Johnnie Sinclair, who was a bit simple and slow. When the tirl (mill wheel) refused to move he would take a "teengs o' brands[1]" and run out and throw it in the water that flowed under the mill. This was to make "knappy", a trow or water spirit, let go of the wheel. He also claimed that he saw the fairies leading foals and prancing about on the mill green in the winter evenings.

Billy Spence of Gyron in Birsay had trouble with the fairies. One night when he was going home from the Barony he past the Well o' Keldereddie, close to the south end of the Hundland Loch. The fairies would trip him up, and then they would laugh at him. He stood up again, but wallop, he was on his back again to more choruses of laughter from the fairies.

[1] *Burning straw or heather held in a pair of tongs.*

John Spence, Overbist. Birsay, "Klik Mills, Birsay, and the Fairies", Vol . II, pt . III 1909 129-132.

A young man from the farm of Sowie in Sandwick was to be married. He was carried to Sule Skerry by the trows and brought back again after what he thought was only a few hours. His friends told him that he had been missing for seven years. His bride-to-be had given him up for dead and had married another man. Strange to say, he was all covered in hair when he returned so that his neighbours had difficulty recognising him.

William Smith 3 Newark, Sandwick, "Trows in Sandwick, Orkney" Vol. VII, pt . III 1914, 98-99.

A child left with a woman went out one night during a snow storm. It returned quite dry, but was now an imbecile. It was thought to be the work of the fairies.

A midwife spent the night with a mother-to-be, but in the morning it was discovered that the child had been born and stolen by the fairies.

Fairies were thought to live at Estaquoy in Houton and in a fairy knowe at Scoradale, Orphir. Fairies were seen in the Fidge of Swanbister, Orphir, with "nice polled heads".

Vol.I, pt . VI I 1908, 247.

Ernest Marwick Papers, Orkney Archives of the Orkney Library, D31

An old woman who lived at Costa, Birsay was a local midwife. She thought that the fairies had power at night. When she was called on to help a woman after dark, she carried a glowing peat in the tongs in front of her.

D31/1, file 2.

There was a man from Papa Westray, and he returned from the whaling for his daughter's wedding. He brewed very strong ale by steeping two lots of malt in the same water. Some of the old men who drank the ale at the wedding were carried away by the trows. They returned after a years absence.

D31/1, file 5.

A man was setting traps for rabbits on the links at Melsetter, Hoy. He saw a huge giant and ran home and refused to return there for the rest of the winter.

D31/1, file 5.

There was a green grassy knowe by the pond at South Tuan, Skelwick, Westray, that was the home of the fairies. A field called Savvoquoy was their field, and children were warned not to roll down the banks there, or tread on a paddostools (toadstools) as the fairies used them as tables, and danced on them in the moonlight. They were said to dress all in green and were no bigger than a thimble. If you stood by the pond at South Tuan you could hear the fairies humming.

The Skelwick fairies came from Rousay on a simman rope. They settled in the old Picts houses at the shore below Garth. An old woman said that the fairies took over after the Picts had left.

D31/1, file 6.

The area around the loch called the Water of Hoy was the haunt of a water horse. It was a lovely looking horse who tried to lure people onto its back and then plunged into the water to drown them. It also haunted the Little Loch on the slope of the hill at Runsigill in Rackwick. Here it waited for victims using the hill road to Longhope. A water horse also haunted the Pegal Burn. Its eyesight was keener at night, and it could spot his victims as they approached the burn from either side. It always met them at the brig that crosses the burn. There was also a water horse on the little island of Rysa Little and in the Loch of Knitchen, Rousay.

D31/1, file 1.

The Loch of Knitchen in Rousay had a water horse. It was a beautiful black horse, and it would leave the loch when the neighbouring farmers had their animals on the hill. The water horse would join the herd, but it never let itself be caught. In another version the horse would let itself be caught, but anyone who got on its back was carried into the loch and drowned.

"An Orkney Anthology" 1991, 274.

An old woman was busy raising peats when she found that she was surrounded by fairies. She was frightened, but she knew what to do. She crossed herself and said a prayer. She was surprised to see that it hadn't worked and the fairies were coming closer. She was a forceful woman, and she acted in character, swearing at the fairies. No sooner were the oaths out of her mouth than the fairies vanished.

"An Orkney Anthology" 1991, 280.

A farmer on Sanday was wakened one night at 3 o'clock by a little man who stood in front of the box bed. The little fellow asked for the loan of a "piftan fiv". The farmer didn't know what he meant, and he grunted that he had no intention of getting out of his warm bed, but told his visitor to look for it himself. The little fellow searched until he found what he wanted, a sifting sieve. When he found it he disappeared with it in a blue flame that shot up through the smoke hole of the roof.

"An Orkney Anthology" 1991, 267.

BBC Radio Orkney Archives

There was once a farmer who lived at Sholtisquoy in North Ronaldsay. The house was built low down, under the ground a bit, so the window was at ground level. This was to keep the house warm in the cold winters. When the old man went out at night he used to shoo the trows away, in case he stood on one for they were very small. He would go out to his barn at night to thresh his sheaves of corn. He would knock all the grain from one of the sheaves with the flail, and then tie the straw up into a neat bundle. He would then say: "All like this", then leave the barn. His wife would put a dish of porridge in the barn, and the cruisie lamp was left burning. In the morning all the sheaves were threshed and the straw tied up into neat bundles. The dish of porridge was empty, for it was the payment to the trows for their work. They stopped helping the man after the lighthouse was lit. The man thought the flashing light scared them away.

Willie Thomson, Neven, North Ronaldsay. "Trows and their Mischief", Tape TA/590.

A North Ronaldsay mother was sure that her bairn had been stolen by the trows and a changeling left in its place. It would eat plenty, but it never grew. It was also very bad tempered. She asked a wise woman for her advice, and she said that she should make a pot of porridge, but to put something into the pot. She had to make sure that the changeling saw her do it. She did as she was told, and the changeling sat up and stared at her. She tried to force the bairn to eat the porridge, but it became very frightened. She then produced a cross, made from a certain wood, and held it up to the changeling. She held the dish of porridge in one hand, and the cross in the other, and she ordered it to eat the porridge. It screamed and leapt up the chimney and was gone. The woman's own bairn was returned to her in about an hour.

Willie Thomson, Neven, North Ronaldsay, "Changelings", Tape TA/590.

Notes and Sources

Abbreviations

O.L.M. Old-Lore Miscellany of Orkney, Shetland, Caithness and Sutherland. The year given is the one in which it was published.

P.O.A.S. Proceedings of the Orkney Antiquarian Society.

S.A.N.N.Q The Scottish Antiquary or Northern Notes and Queries.

ASSIPATTLE AND THE MESTER STOORWORM: Ernest Marwick, "The Folklore Of Orkney And Shetland" 1975, 20, 139-144. Walter Traill Dennison, S.A.N.N.Q. Vol. V 1891, 130-131. Reprinted in "Orkney Folklore and Traditions" 1961, 8-10. "Orkney Folklore & Sea Legends" 1995, 22-25. Walter Traill Dennison. "Assipattle and the Mester Stoorworm" in Sir George Douglas, "Scottish Fairy and Folk Tales" 1893, 58-72 reprinted in Walter Traill Dennison, "Orkney Folklore & Sea Legends" 1995, 104-118. In this version Assiepattle has a sister who goes to the castle to work for the princess. The princess has a wicked step mother, who is the lover of the spae man. The spae man's advice to give the princess to the Stoorworm is a ploy to get rid of her. Assipattle's sister tells him of the plots he chases the spae man on Teatgong and kills him with the magic sword. See also Ernest Marwick, "An Orkney Anthology" 1991, 282.

THE CAITHNESS GIANT; Ernest Marwick, "An Orkney Anthology" 1991, 259. See also Mrs Johina J. Leith "The Hugboy" in A.J. Bruford and D.A. MacDonald "Scottish Traditional Tales" 1994, 295-296 (recordings from The School of Scottish Studies archive).

WHY THE SEA IS SALT: Ernest Marwick, "An Anthology of Orkney Verse" 1949, 16-20 (this story was recorded as a song called "The Lay of Grotti"). Ernest Marwick, "The Folklore of Orkney and Shetland" 1975, 32. See also O.L.M. Vol. III, pts. I and IV 1910, 8-10, 139-150, 237-253. Howie Firth, "Tales of Long Ago" 1986, 24-28. Originally a song, it was also well known as a folk tale in Orkney. In Orkney the names of the giant women changed to Grotti-Fenni and Grotti-Menni. In Fair Isle they were known as Grotti Finnie and Lucky Minnie, and were used to frighten children. They were also turned into witches in some versions.

THE MOTHER OF THE SEA: Walter Traill Dennison, S.A.N.N.Q. Vol. V 1891 70-71. Reprinted in "Orkney Folklore and Traditions" 1961, 6-7. "Orkney Folklore & Sea Legends" 1995, 20-21. Ernest Marwick, "The Folklore of Orkney and Shetland" 1975, 19-20.

HOW THE MERMAID GOT HER TAIL: Walter Traill Dennison, S.A.N.N.Q. Vol. VI 1892, 116-117. Reprinted in "Orkney Folklore and Traditions" 1961, 23-24. "Orkney Folklore & Sea Legends" 1995, 39-40.

THE TROWS OF TROWIE GLEN: Ernest Marwick, "An Orkney Anthology" 1991, 271. Original version told by John Bremner, amongst Ernest Marwick's papers in the Orkney Archives of the Orkney Library, D31/1, file 1. The latter is the version used, as it is given in full. Since published in John Bremner, "Hoy, the dark enchanted isle" 1997, 95-97.

THE LOST GIRL: James Henderson, "Tocher no. 26" 1977, 95-96. School of Scottish Studies publication. "The Magic Island" in A.J. Bruford and D.A. MacDonald, "Scottish Traditional Tales" 1994, 370-372, (recordings from The School Of Scottish Studies archive)

THE SELKIE WIFE: J.A. Pottinger, O.L.M. Vol I, pt. V 1908, 173-175.

THE FIN FOLK AND THE MILL OF SKAILL: George Marwick, "Notes on Orcadian Folk-Lore", 1884. Unpublished paper from Stromness Museum's archive. Also copy amongst Ernest Marwick's papers in the Orkney Archives of the Orkney Library, D31/ 4. See also Howie Firth, "Tales of Long Ago" 1986, 35-39. This story stresses the importance of concealing your name.

THE STANDING STONES: The Yetnasteen, Hugh Marwick, "Antiquarian Notes on Rousay", P.O.A.S. Vol. II 1923/1924. 15. The Stone of Quoybune, G.F. Black, "County Folk-Lore Vol.III, Orkney & Shetland Islands" 1903, 3-4. The Watch Stone, Peter Leith, Langbigging, Stenness, pers comm. The North Ronaldsay Stone, "Legend of N. Ron. Standing Stone" Willie Thomson, Neven, North Ronaldsay, BBC Radio Orkney Archive recording TA/591. The Ring of Brodgar, local tradition, confirmed by Peter Leith, Langbigging, Stenness.

JOCK IN THE KNOWE: Duncan J. Robertson, "Orkney Folk-Lore", P.O.A.S. Vol. I 1922/23, 37-38. "Orkney Folk-Lore Notes" O.L.M. Vol II, pt. II 1909, 108.

HOW TAM SCOTT LOST HIS SIGHT; Walter Traill Dennison, S.A.N.N.Q. Vol. VII 1893, 115-117. Reprinted in "Orkney Folklore and Traditions" 1961, 51-54. "Orkney Folklore & Sea Legends" 1995, 67-70. See also Nancy and W. Towrie Cutt, "The Hogboon of Hell, and other strange Orkney tales" 1979, 130-133.

THE ROUSAY CHANGELING: Duncan J. Robertson, "Orkney Folk-Lore" P.O.A.S. Vol. I 1922/23, 38. See also Ernest Marwick, "The Folklore of Orkney and Shetland" 1975, 83.

THE CITY AT THE BOTTOM OF THE SEA: Walter Traill Dennison, S.A.N.N.Q. Vol. VII 1893, 20-24. Reprinted in "Orkney Folklore and Traditions" 1961, 34-43. "Orkney Folklore & Sea Legends" 1995, 50-58. See also Howie Firth "Tales of Long Ago" 1986, 18-23.

THE SELKIE MAN: Irvine Family Genealogical Group, Third Quarter 1994, 22-23. Canadian publication. The story is given by Dean J. Irvine from family documents. Given as a true story, but is likely to be based on a local folk tradition.

TAM BICHAN AND THE TROWS: Dr John Tait, "Tam Bichan and the Trows", article in "The Orcadian" newspaper, January 20 1943, 5.

THE GIANTS OF HOY; Jo Ben, "A Description of the Orchadian Islands" 1529. Translated by Margaret Hunter, 1987, 17-18. From manuscripts in the National Library of Scotland. The date 1529 is too early for some of the information in the text, more likely to be mid to late 16th century.

THE SHETLAND FIN WIFE: Walter Traill Dennison, S.A.N.N.Q. Vol. V 1891, 170-171. Reprinted in "Orkney Folklore and Traditions" 1961, 20-21. "Orkney Folklore & Sea Legends" 1995, 36-38.

THE HOGBOON OF HELLIHOWE: Hugh Marwick, "Antiquarian Notes on Sanday", P.O.A.S. Vol. I 1922/23, 28. Ernest Marwick, "The Folklore of Orkney and Shetland" 1975, 42. "An Orkney Anthology" 1991, 268. Nancy and W. Towrie Cutt, "The Hogboon of Hell, and other strange Orkney stories; 1979."

THE EVERLASTING BATTLE: Ernest Marwick, "An Anthology of Orkney Verse" 1949, 21-22. Written by Bragi the Skald, cg. 835-900 AD. See also Howie Firth, "Tales of Long Ago" 1986, 29-34. The theme of the song seems to be a well known folk tale.

LADY ODIVERE: Walter Traill Dennison, "The Play o' De Lathie Odivere" S.A.N.N.Q. Vol VIII 1894, 53-58. Reprinted in "Orkney Folklore & Sea Legends" 1995, 88-103. See also G.F. Black, "County Folk-Lore Vol. III, Orkney and Shetland Islands" 1903, 235-248. Ernest Marwick, "An Anthology of Orkney Verse" 1949, 54-64. Similar story to the song "The Great Selkie of Sule Skerry", in Ernest Marwick, "An Anthology of Orkney Verse" 1949, 65-67. Originally sung as a song, but it was also known as a folk tale. Also recorded as a tale in Caithness.

THE TROWIE SNUFF-BOX: John Spence, O.L.M. Vol. II, pt. III 1909, 131. Ernest Marwick, "The Folklore of Orkney and Shetland" 1975, 36 "An Orkney Anthology" 1991, 60-61.

THE SUITER FROM THE SEA: James Henderson, "Tocher no. 26" 1977, 100-101. School of Scottish Studies publication. See also "Keeping Out The Sea Man" in A.J. Bruford and D.A. Macdonald "Scottish Traditional Tales" 1994, 363-364. (recordings from The School of Scottish Studies archive).

THE SANDWICK FAIRIES; William Smith, Newark, Sandwick, "Sandwick Trows" O.L.M. Vol IV, pt 1 1911, 2-3.

THE WATER TROWS: William Smith, Newark, Sandwick, "Sandwick Trows" O.L.M. Vol IV, pt 1 1911, 3. The dialect used by the trows in this story was, "Strae's gae'n." "Sit still and warm thee wame. Weel kens thoo strae canna gang." The story can also be found in Ernest Marwick, "An Orkney Anthology" 1991, 264.

HILDA-LAND: Walter Traill Dennison, S.A.N.N.Q. Vol VII 1893, 113-115. Reprinted in "Orkney Folklore and Traditions" 1961, 47-51. "Orkney Folklore & Sea Legends" 1995, 64-67. See also Nancy and W. Towrie Cutt, "The Hogboon of Hell, and other strange Orkney tales" 1979, 147-151. "The Faber Book of Northern Folktales" 1980 ed. Kevin Crossley-Holland, 85-89.

THE CHANGELING TWIN: R. Menzies Fergusson, "Rambles in the Far North" 1884, 219-221.

THE HOLMS OF IRE: Ernest Marwick, "The Folklore of Orkney and Shetland" 1975, 29.

MANSIE O' FEA: Compiled from two sources, William Smith, "Mansie o' Kierfa and his Fairy Wife" O.L.M. Vol VI, pt. I 1913, 19-21. George Marwick, "Mansie o' Fea" in unpublished paper "Notes on Orcadian Folk-Lore" 1884. From Stromness Museum's archive, also copy amongst Ernest Marwick's papers in the Orkney Archives of the Orkney Library, D31/4.

KATE CRACKERNUTS: Duncan J. Robertson, Longman's Magazine, XIII; Folk-Lore, 299-301. Reprinted in Katharine M. Briggs, "A Dictionary of British Folk-Tales in the English Language" 1970, 344- 346. There seems to have been a mistake in the original text, as it gives the king's daughter the name of Kate, yet for the rest of the text, it is the queens daughter who is called Kate. I have changed it so that the story makes sense, my thanks to Prof. Bo Almqvist for his advice.

THE CHANGELING: R. Menzies Fergusson, "Rambles in the Far North" 1884, 222-223.

THE HOUSE OF THE DEAD: William Smith, "The Quholmsley Dog, etc", O.L.M. Vol VII, pt. III 1914, 98.

THE DEATH OF THE FIN KING: George Marwick, in unpublished paper "Notes on Orcadian Folk-Lore" 1884. From Stromness Museum's archive, also copy amongst Ernest Marwick's papers in the Orkney Archives of the Orkney Library, D31/4. George Marwick, "The Death of the Fin King, an Orcadian legend" in "The Orkney Herald" newspaper, Wednesday, December 2, 1891, 7.

THE FAIRIES FISHING TRIP: John Dass, "Tocher no. 26" 1977, 103. School of Scottish Studies publication.

THE BROONIE OF COPINSAY: Ernest Marwick, "The Folklore of Orkney and Shetland" 1975, 148-150. Also from notes among Ernest Marwick's papers in the Orkney Archives of the Orkney Library, D31, recorded from "W.D.", Deerness. I have used both versions, though I favour the version in the notes.

THE GOOD NEIGHBOURS OF GREENIE HILL: D.S., "Greenie Hill and the Good Neighbours" O.L.M. Vol. III, pt. IV, 1910 209-210.

THE FAIRY BATTLE: D.S., "Greenie Hill and the Good Neighbours" O.L.M. Vol. III, pt. IV 1910, 210-211.

THE BRECKNESS MERMAID: R. Menzies Fergusson,"Rambles in the Far North" 1884, 237-240. Reprinted as "The Mermaid-Bride" in "Peace's Orkney and Shetland Almanac" 1922, 117-118. I had already called this book by that name before I found this story.

DAVIE O' TEEVETH: Magnus Flett, "A Link With Other Days, The Prophet And The Wee Folk" O.L.M. Vol. V, pt. III 1910, 116-119.

BUILDING THE CATHEDRAL: In Ernest Marwick's papers in the Orkney Archives of the Orkney Library, D31/1, file 5.

THE STOLEN WINDING SHEET: Walter Traill Dennison, "The Stown Windin' sheet" in "The Orcadian Sketch Book" 1880, 35-40. Reprinted in "Orcadian Sketches" 1903, 17-24. See also Nancy and W. Towrie Cutt, "The Hogboon of Hell, and other strange Orkney Tales" 1979, 80-86.

THE EVIE MAN'S DANCE: W.R. Mackintosh, "Around The Orkney Peat-Fires" 1957, 299. Originally appeared in serial form in "The Orcadian" newspaper at the turn of the 20th century. The book has been reprinted many times, the 1957 edition being the sixth.

BORAY ISLE; John Kerr, "Orkney and the Orcadians" in "Good Words", September 1, 1865. Reprinted in "Peace's Orkney and Shetland Almanac" 1882, 136. Also exists as a song by Alice L. Dundas in John Gunn, "The Orkney Book" 1909, 403-407.

THE TROWS OF HUIP: Ernest Marwick, "The Folklore of Orkney and Shetland" 1975, 37. "An Orkney Anthology" 1991, 263. See also Ernest Marwick's papers in the Orkney Archives of the Orkney Library, D31. School of Scottish Studies recording of James Logie, Stronsay, SA 1967/110.

HETHER BLETHER; Duncan J. Robertson, "Orkney Folk-Lore", P.O.A.S. Vol. I 1922/23, 40. "Orkney Folk-Lore Notes". O.L.M. Vol. II pt. II 1909, 105.

TAMMY HAY AND THE FAIRIES; J.T. Smith Leask, "Tammy Hay and the Fairies", O.L.M. Vol. III, pt. I 1910, 28-33.

THE NUCKLAVEE: Walter Traill Dennison, S.A.N.N.Q. Vol. V 1891, 131-133. Reprinted in Sir George Douglas, "Scottish Fairy and Folk Tales" 1893, 160-163. "Orkney Folklore and Traditions" 1961, 11-14. "Orkney Folklore & Sea Legends" 1995, 26-29.

THE FAIRIES AND THE VIKINGS: Duncan J. Robertson, "Orkney Folk-Lore", P.O.A.S. Vol. I 1922/23, 39.

THE BRIDE OF RAMRAY: George Marwick, in unpublished paper "The Bride of Ramrie" 1894. Stromness Museum's archive, also copy amongst Ernest Marwick's papers in the Orkney Archives of the Orkney Library, D31/4. I have used the correct island spelling of "Ramray".

THE TROW'S CURSE: D.S. "Orkney Mound-Lore", O.L.M. Vol IV pt. III, 1911, 116-117. See also Ernest Marwick, "The Folklore of Orkney and Shetland" 1975, p41.

PEERIE FOOL: Duncan J. Robertson, "Orkney Folk-Lore", P.O.A.S. Vol. I 1922/23, 41-42. Reprinted in G.F. Black, "County Folk-Lore Vol. III, Orkney and Shetland" 1903, 222-226. See also Ernest Marwick's "The Folklore of Orkney and Shetland" 1975, 144-146. "An Orkney Anthology" 1991, 290-292. C.M. Costie, "Orkney Dialect Tales" 1976, 72-78. This is two stories in one. The "Peerie Fool" part is similar to the Grimm brothers "Rumpelstiltskin", and an English tale, "Tom Tit Tot". The second part concerning the giant and the caisies of grass, is similar to a tale from Norway, "The Three Sisters who were Entrapped into a Mountain". It can be found, along with "Tom Tit Tot", in "The Faber Book of Northern Folk-Tales", 1980, 49-55, 123-127.

THE TROW WIFE: Duncan J. Robertson, "Orkney Folk-Lore", P.O.A.S. Vol. I 1922/23, 38. "Orkney Folk-Lore Notes", O.L.M. Vol. II, pt. II 1909, 108-109. Ernest Marwick, "An Orkney Anthology" 1991, 263.

URSILLA AND THE SELKIE MAN: Walter Traill Dennison, S.A.N.N.Q. Vol. VII 1893, 175-176. Reprinted in G.F. Black, "County Folk-Lore Vol. III, Orkney and Shetland Islands" 1903, 176-179. "Orkney Folklore and Traditions" 1961, 68-70. "Orkney Folklore & Sea Legends" 1953 84-87.

THE DANCERS UNDER THE HILL: J.T. Smith Leask T "Tammy Hay and the Fairies", O.L.M. Vol. III, pt. II 1910, 30-31. The mound at Howe was excavated between 1978-82, and was found to contain a large broch and village, built on top of a Neolithic tomb. The author started his archaeological career on this excavation, but found no fairies!

HOW THE FIN FOLK LOST EYNHALLOW: Walter Traill Dennison, S.A.N.N.Q. Vol. VII 1893, 117-120. Reprinted in "Orkney Folklore and Traditions" 1961, 54-61. "Orkney Folklore & Sea Legends" 1995, 71-77. See also Nancy and W. Towrie Cutt, "The Hogboon of Hell, and other strange Orkney tales" 1979, 124-129. It was said that no cat, rat or mouse could live on Eynhallow. Stones from the island were placed under the threshold of houses in Kirkwall to keep vermin out. It was also claimed that earth from Eynhallow was carted to Westness in Rousay, and spread to a depth of six inches over the stackyard. This was to protect the grain stacks from vermin.

THE MIDNIGHT RIDE: Anonymous letter to The Orcadian, March 27, 1924. Reprinted in Ernest Marwick, "An Orkney Anthology" 1991, 273.

THE SELKIE WIFE OF WESTNESS: Walter Traill Dennison, S.A.N.N.Q. Vol. VII 1893, 173-175. Reprinted in G.F. Black, "County Folk-Lore Vol. III, Orkney and Shetland Islands" 1903. 173-176. "Orkney Folklore and Traditions" 1961, 64-67. "Orkney Folklore & Sea Legends" 1995, 81-84.

THE FARMER AND THE TROW SERVANT: Willie Thomson, Neven, North Ronaldsay, "Story of Farmer & Trow", BBC Radio Orkney archive recording, TA/591.

THE MAN FROM NOWHERE: Anonymous article entitled "The Fairies" in "The Orcadian" newspaper of March 13 1924, 3. See also Ernest Marwick, "An Orkney Anthology" 1991, 288-289.

THE DEAD WIFE WITH THE FAIRIES: Sydney Scott, "The Dead Wife Among the Fairies", in A.J. Bruford and D.A. Macdonald, "Scottish Traditional Tales" 1994, 357. (recordings from The School of Scottish Studies archives). Mary A. Scott, "Island saga, the story of North Ronaldsay" No publication date given, 155-156

THE HOUSE ON SULE SKERRY: George Marwick, unpublished paper, "Notes on Orcadian Folk-Lore" 1884, Stromness Museum's archive, copy amongst Ernest Marwick's papers in the-Orkney Archives of the Orkney Library, D31/4.

THE DEATH OF THE MAINLAND TROWS: R. Menzies Fergusson, "Rambles in the Far North" 1884, 230-233. Ernest Marwick, "An Orkney Anthology" 1991, 271-272. I have used Marwick's version as Fergusson's contains dubious verses and what seems to be additions to the story.

THE MERMAID BRIDE: Walter Traill Dennison, S.A.N.N.Q. Vol. VI 1892. 118-121. Reprinted in "Orkney Folklore and Traditions" 1961, 26-32. "Orkney Folklore & Sea Legends" 1995. 42-47. See also Nancy and W. Towrie Cutt, "The Hogboon of Hell, and other strange Orkney tales" 1979, 108-113.